DISOBEDIENCE

LOIS D. BROWN

WISE WOLF BOOKS
an imprint of Wolfpack Publishing
wisewolfbooks.com

WISE WOLF
BOOKS

WISE WOLF BOOKS
An Imprint of Wolfpack Publishing
wisewolfbooks.com

Cover design by Wise Wolf Books

ISBN 978-1-953944-47-4 (paperback)
ISBN 978-1-953944-46-7 (ebook)
Library of Congress Control Number: 2022935056

First Edition: May 2022

PREACHER DOCKET'S RULES FOR SAINTLY YOUTH

1. No Kissing
2. No Lying
3. No Interrupting Sabbath Service
4. No Fraternizing with Strangers
5. No Pilfering
6. No Hunting on the Sabbath
7. No Loitering After Dark
8. No Animals Indoors
9. No Parties
10. No Talking Past Midnight
11. No Eavesdropping
12. No Running in the Streets
13. No Napping
14. No Heavy Drinking
15. No Gluttony
16. No Profanity
17. No Horse Riding on the Sabbath
18. No Addressing Adults by their First Name
19. No Boys in Girls' Bedrooms

20. No Money Hoarding
21. No Forming Clubs
22. No Horseplay
23. No Loaded Guns in Town
24. No Shooting Varmints

DISOBEDIENCE

1. NO KISSING

EVER SINCE RUTH Ivins tackled Clyde Hampton during a game of Red Rover in grammar school, I've wanted to kiss her. Truth is, Ruth happens to be the prettiest girl in Docketville. Clyde, on the other hand, is as nasty and ugly as an angry rattler. If I saw him getting eaten by a cougar in the hills above town, I'd sit down, get comfortable, and watch the show.

I know that's not something a good Bible-believing boy would do, but neither is waiting in a stable for a kiss, which I happen to be doing— except that I can hardly sit still. I'm scared Ruth will come, and worried that she won't. My breath comes out short and fast, like it does after chasing chickens all afternoon. A horse fly lands on my neck and takes a bite. If cursing wasn't such a sin, I'd let out a few choice words.

The door creaks open, and I nearly fall off the bale of hay I'm sitting on. Is it her?

My best friend Frank said she wanted to

come, but I didn't totally believe him. I stand up, my tongue parched as jerky. I'm certain I won't be good at this romance stuff even though I'm well into my thirteenth year. I've never even held a girl's hand.

"Dillan?" Ruth whispers. She doesn't see me in the corner, which is a good thing because my jaw is hanging wide open. I'm sure I look as stupid as a treed squirrel.

"Over here," I say.

She spies me by the pitchforks and shovels. I wish she'd smile but her face is all business. Her skirt drags hay from the floor as she walks. I lean my shoulder into the weathered wall planks and fold my arms so she can't see them shaking.

"Frank said you wanted to see me."

Ruth's hair is pulled back in a golden braid that reaches down to her lower back, and her hands are as red as a rooster's comb. She's come from washing dishes at Preacher Docket's Hotel and Diner. That's been her family's community job for years. They're lucky—my family has charge of the swine, and nothing unhinges the preacher of Docketville like a dirty pig pen. Well, nothing except for a youngster in his flock breaking one of the Rules for Saintly Youth.

"Frank only said I wanted to see you?" I ask. "Nothing else?"

The last of the evening sun dips below the stable's window, and her face fades slightly into the shadows.

"That's all Frank said," she answers.

Confused, I gawk at her.

"Listen, Dillan, what's going on? I've got a

mess of pots to finish up before Preacher Docket gets back from his trip to Riverdale."

"Frank didn't mention...anything 'bout..." My words dry up. Frank's been playing me for a fool, telling me Ruth was sweet on me.

She inches toward me—closer than she's ever stood before. Her mouth is upturned in a slightly wicked smile. "Why, Dillan," she whispers, "I think you're blushing. Makes me think you might have lured me here to take advantage of being alone with me."

Ruth's breath lands hot on my neck. I don't dare swallow; afraid I might choke on the air that's as thick as mush. Outside, a dog barks fiercely.

"I'd never take advantage of you." Drops of sweat cover my forehead.

She puts her hand on the front pocket of my denim overalls over my chest. My heart feels like it could jump right out of my skin.

"Oh, I do remember now," she says, "Frank may have said something about a kiss."

More barking erupts outside.

A foot shorter than me, Ruth has to lean her neck back to look me in the face. Her eyes are a bright blue, and they make me not care that she's been pulling my leg.

I unfold my arms, suddenly aware how dirty my hands are. Where should I put them?

For the kiss, I was planning on holding her around the waist, but my filthy fingers might leave a mark on her clothes. I swing my arms in front and then in back, trying to figure out the best position.

She laughs. It's sweet, not the kind people use when making fun.

More than anything I wish she'd move her face closer to mine. Then it hits me—that's my job! Taking a deep breath, I forget my hands and breach the last few inches between us. I'm big for my age—nearly six feet tall—and it comes with some disadvantages. I must crouch to line my lips up with hers.

The stable doors crash open.

"Dillan Burnes!" shouts Preacher Docket. "Get your hands off of that virtuous pearl this second!"

I leap backward, smacking into the wall behind me. No question about it, I'd have preferred if the devil himself had barged in. Things might not look so grim if he did.

Ruth covers her mouth with both hands to stifle a scream. I wish there was something I could do, something to make her feel better, but there's nothing.

The preacher hands his black hat and horse's reins to Dirk Hampton, Clyde's dad and Preacher Docket's traveling companion, and takes Ruth by the shoulders, jolting her.

"Miss Ivins, it pains me to ask, but did that boy defile you? You must tell the truth, or you shall never rid yourself of the temptation of prurience. I know this is not of your doing."

"He didn't...defile me." Ruth's voice is small. At that moment it's hard for me to imagine her tackling anyone, let alone Clyde Hampton in grammar school. She seems as tender as a willow branch.

"Don't lie!" The preacher shakes her back and forth so hard her teeth chatter.

"I...fell down and bumped my chin," she insists. "Dillan helped me up and was making sure I wasn't hurt."

Preacher Docket stops jolting her.

It sounds strange, but I hope Preacher Docket gets his whip out. A quick whipping would be much better than one of his "Bible punishments", as he calls them.

"Dirk," the preacher says calmly, "do you still have those shears in your saddle bags?"

"Yes, sir."

"Did you have a chance to sharpen them?"

"No, sir."

Preacher Docket sighs. "Never mind, they'll still do." He holds out an open hand. Dirk fumbles in his bags a moment and then pulls out a pair of hand-held brush clippers. The preacher takes Ruth's long braid and places it in between the dull blades. Stunned, I tell myself he won't really do it.

"Do you recall Apostle Paul from the Bible, Miss Ivins?" Preacher Docket asks Ruth.

"Yes, sir."

"And do you remember what he told the heretics of his time?"

"Not exactly." Ruth shivers.

"He told them it was a shame for a woman to be shorn or shaven. It was the mark of a sinner."

Ruth whimpers.

The dull blades make a sickly sound as they cut into her hair. My knees knock together, and I wish a hundred times over I'd never wanted a kiss.

It takes a full minute of gnawing, but at last a foot and a half of her braid falls to the ground. Ruth reaches up and runs her hands through her yellow hair, the ends of which now hit her shoulders. A soft cry escapes her mouth.

"I'll talk to your father later," Preacher Docket says to her. "For now, you get home. Don't forget, Miss Ivins, the Lord already has chosen a deserving husband for you, and he is in no way, shape, or form this sinful young man."

Ruth pulls her skirts up and rushes out the door. But she's not quick enough. I see tears falling from her eyes as fast as a July rain.

"Dirk," Preacher Docket says, "go fetch Nurse Mabel and tell her to meet me at Dillan Burnes' house within the hour. It's an emergency."

"Sure thing." With that, Dirk saunters from the stable, leaving me alone with the preacher. We've only been in the same room together by ourselves once before, and that was months ago. Before Pa died.

I'd gone to the community storehouse to pick up our family's allotment of flour, baking soda, and the like, when I'd seen a big box of peppermint sticks. They looked so tempting. I admit, a little voice inside my head told me not to do it, but I wanted one so bad my mouth watered. I took a red and white striped stick and put it in the bottom of my basket only to turn around and see Preacher Docket staring at me. Within seconds he had his belt off and was giving me a licking. I still have scars.

Unfortunately, those whip marks hadn't stopped me from trying to kiss Ruth today.

"Dillan," Preacher Docket says, "I knew you were a thief, but I never took you for a womanizer as well. These are serious sins, boy. The young women in our community need to be warned. You're a danger to them."

Without another word, he walks away.

2. NO LYING

USING WELL WATER, I clean my hands—
something I should have done before Ruth came
to the barn. I wish to high heaven that I didn't
have to go home. But where else is there to go? It
takes two weeks to walk to the closest town from
here. I wipe my hands on my overalls and drag
myself down the road.

"Ahhhooo."

The sound makes me jump. What kind of
sick animal is that? A bush moves. Hiding
behind it is my friend Frank. He's tall, but I still
have a few inches on him. And he's skinnier
than a fence post. He waves and frowns, the
corners of his mouth pull down his white,
freckly cheeks.

"What happened in there?" he asks, anxiously
running his hand through his wiry red hair.

"I don't want to talk 'bout it," I answer.

"Why didn't you two come out of the stable
when I warned you?"

The fool is talking nonsense. "You never warned me, you fed me to the wolves!"

"Not true," says Frank, his hands fly into the air. "I was barking like a mad dog trying to warn you that the preacher got back early. You two must have been awful busy doing who-knows-what not to hear me."

I want to kick myself in the hind end. I'd heard the barking plain as day but hadn't paid much notice, not with Ruth standing so close. I could have saved her from humiliation. That's the last time I let my lips do the thinking instead of my brain.

"We didn't kiss," I say, "and I didn't hear you." The second part's a fib, which means I just fell prey to breaking another of Preacher Docket's rules, but I have no hope for salvation anyhow after what I did in the barn.

Frank looks at me funny, shrugs his shoulders, and spits. "Well, you don't look any worse for wear. Preacher Docket didn't teach you a lesson with his whip?"

"No," I say, "and I need to get home. Ma's expecting me."

I don't tell him about who else is waiting for me, namely the preacher and Nurse Mabel, who, as it happens, I hate almost as much as Clyde Hampton.

———

I take a deep breath before opening the door to my house. When I see there's only Ma and my little brother Josh seated around the dinner table, my heart sinks. Sometimes I still forget Pa is gone.

Josh wiggles his dark eyebrows at me and laughs. With his pale skin and licorice-colored hair, some might think he looks a bit sinister. Nothing is further from the truth. He's quick with a joke and generous with his smiles.

"You're late," says Ma. "What's been keeping you? The stew's gone cold."

Ma has a way of making me feel guilty without ever raising her voice or touching a switch. Josh, who just turned nine, says it's because Ma can talk down a rabid dog. He's probably right.

"Sorry, Ma," I say. "I had a problem in the town stables with the horses." It's not exactly a lie. Just a half-truth.

"Whose horses?" asks Ma, confused. Our family doesn't own any.

"The horses in the town stable," I answer, doing my best not to let my eyes drop to the floor. A good steady gaze is the best way to show innocence.

"What were you doing there?" Ma stands up. After my last growth spurt, I've got her by six inches.

A pounding on the front door stops me from answering her. Everyone knows a visitor is never good news this time of night. My knees are weak.

"Get the door, Dillan," Ma says.

I don't move.

"Dillan, answer it!" Ma's face is turning as purple as a newly picked beet.

I do what I'm told. On the porch stand two

figures—a man dressed in black, and a ball-shaped woman in a white smock. Well, more like gray.

"Hello, Dillan," says Preacher Docket, like he hasn't seen me in weeks. "Is your mother home?"

Next to the preacher, Nurse Mabel clicks her tongue and scolds me with her dull, gray eyes. In her pudgy hands she holds a large, brown glass bottle. There's not a kid in Docketville who hasn't been forced to swallow some of her nasty home-made medicine at one time or another. She teaches obedience as fervently as Preacher Docket does. Just in her own way.

"Move over, boy, and let us in." Preacher Docket pushes me aside and walks to Ma's rocking chair, the best seat in the house. "This isn't a social call," he says, pursing his lips. "Has your boy told you what he's been doing this evening?"

Ma shakes her head and prods the fire with a poker.

"I didn't have time to explain yet—" I begin, but a powerful glare from Preacher Docket convinces me to shut my mouth.

"You will only speak when you're spoken to," he says. "Do you understand?"

I bow my head in submission and look down at the floor, studying the wood beneath me. How I wish the swells in the grain were ocean waves that could take me away from all of this.

"Mrs. Burnes, your son was seen by my very own eyes taking advantage of a young lady."

Ma gasps.

"Now, in our lovely community, what do you

suppose would happen if we let every disobedient boy gallivant about following his devilish passions?"

Speechless, Ma grips the fire poker until her knuckles turn white.

"I'll tell you what would happen—we'd have carnal chaos." Preacher Docket loves to answer his own questions, especially during his Sunday sermons. "Now, let's not give up on the boy quite yet. Apostle Mathew tells us in the Good Book what to do with young folks who fall into temptation like this."

With that, he opens his extra-large Bible and reads: "*Wherefore if thy hand or foot offend thee, cut them off. It is better to enter into life maimed, rather than having two hands or two feet be cast into everlasting fire.*"

It's a scripture I've heard many times before.

Preacher Docket continues: "*And if thine eye offend thee, pluck it out. It is better to enter into life with one eye, rather than having two eyes be cast into hell fire.*"

The words echo off our empty walls. I don't even remember my little brother is still in the room until Ma calls out his name.

"Josh," she says, "get yourself upstairs."

But my little brother doesn't budge. He glares at the preacher with his coal black eyes, his jaw set in stone. I'm the only one that notices that his bottom lip quivers for a short moment.

It's one thing to let Ma down, but I can't stand the thought that Josh is disappointed in me, too.

"Go!" Ma's voice cracks.

It's like someone lit a match under Josh. He

angrily throws down his napkin and runs up the stairs into our bedroom. Once he's gone, I think of the words of the scripture Preacher Docket read. Did he say something about cutting a person's hands off? My wrists begin to throb.

He wouldn't...would he?

I think back hard, and I don't recall Michael Burton getting anything cut off when he was caught hiding in the school's root cellar with Priscilla Dunley.

"If we'd lived in the olden days," Preacher Docket says, "Dillan's punishment would've been dismemberment."

I don't know what *dismemberment* means, and I'm pretty sure I don't want to.

"But this is 1916, and fortunately the Lord is more compassionate in our era." Turning, he says, "Dillan, take off your shoes."

I follow his orders. Nurse Mabel struggles to bend her plump legs and kneel on the floor next to me, but she finally succeeds. She opens the lid of the brown bottle she's been holding and pulls out the biggest swab I've ever laid eyes on. It's covered in bright purple goo. I'm close enough to read the label—*Gentian Violet*.

She wipes the liquid all over my feet, coating them thickly. I wait for something to happen, thinking it might prickle or sting, but everything feels fine. Maybe this won't be so bad after all.

"Now your hands," commands the preacher.

Nurses Mabel breathes heavily as she raised herself to her feet. I hold my hands out in front of me and the nurse covers them in the same bright liquid. Several drops fall to the floor, making purple circles on the wooden planks.

"Now, close your eyes." Preacher Docket rocks back and forth, humming *Battle Hymn of the Republic*. It's his favorite.

"My eyes?" I ask Nurse Mabel, stepping backward.

The woman speaks for the first time. "Gentian Violet cures thrush in babies. Problem is," she smiles, "it stains the skin mighty bad. The color lasts for weeks."

Stains?

"Close your eyes," repeats Preacher Docket.

I shut them tightly and wait. The wetness on my face makes me cold. Nurse Mabel wipes the medicine from the top of my forehead down to my chin, swabbing extra hard on my cheeks. She even puts some on my earlobes. I gag from the smell. I keep my face pinched into a grimace cause my eyes burn like there's a hundred fire ants in them.

"Thank you, Nurse Mabel," says Preacher Docket. "That's good enough for now, unless Dillan doesn't learn his lesson, which would then require us to take more severe measures." I hear him straighten his jacket. "Virginia," he says to Ma, "I recommend a good whipping on your part. You've spared the rod one too many times with your boys."

My eyes are shut tighter than a newborn kitten's so I only hear the preacher and Nurse Mabel leave. Seconds later, Ma's hand is on my arm. She leads me to the kitchen where she pushes my head into the wash bucket. For a moment I think she's going to drown me. Might as well. I'm as good as doomed with purple feet, hands, and face. It's like I've got the plague. Nobody will want to get near me. Especially not Ruth.

Ma pulls my head from the water and starts scrubbing my skin with a bristle brush.

It burns like I'm on fire.

"The man has gone too far," she mutters. "His father would've never done something like this. Oh, how I wish Docket Senior hadn't died. His son is a disgrace to the cloth, and so are all of his so-called rules."

I've never heard my mother bad mouth anything about Preacher Docket before, though I've always known she didn't care for him much compared to his father. She plunges my head back into the bucket. The water soothes my face as it washes away the medicine. How I wish it could wash away my sins too, but I'm afraid those are mine to keep.

3. NO INTERRUPTING SABBATH SERVICE

JOSH'S COUGHING wakes me up. It's not quite as bad as Pa's coughing was before he died, but it's getting worse every day. I pull the quilt over my head and wish I were a hibernating bear. Of course, Ma didn't whip me last night like Preacher Docket told her to, but she did tell me I had to go to church today. I'd rather have gotten a few lashes.

"Josh?" I whisper to the now quiet form lying next to me in bed.

"Yeah?" he answers.

"You awake?"

He rustles under the covers. "No. How 'bout you?"

Pulling the pillow out from under my head, I hit him with it until he starts laughing so hard that the hacking in his lungs comes back.

"Josh, be honest. What does my face look like?"

"Like a big-old blueberry grew right in between your shoulders." Josh muffles a snort.

It took a good scrubbing from Ma before my stained purple skin quieted down to a dull blue. "Do you suppose Ruth will notice?"

"She'd have to be blind if she doesn't. There isn't any way not to." Josh launches into a fit of violent coughs, but this time it doesn't stop. His face turns blue, about the same shade as mine. I whack him on the back five or six times. He looks at me gratefully, but it doesn't seem to help.

I'm about to get out of the sheets and go get Ma when Josh starts to gag.

"Hold on," I tell him. Reaching under the bed, I pull out the thunder pot, which, thankfully, hadn't been used in the night.

Just in time, I set it on his lap, and he empties his stomach into it. Blood is mixed with last night's stew. I turn my face. One thing I know for sure is that I never want to be a doctor. I'd rather clean the community pig pens.

"Sorry," says Josh once he's through. "I'll take care of it."

"No, you won't," I say and shove him back. His body, which was once as muscular as a kid two years his senior, flies back onto the mattress with hardly a thud. "You rest a minute. I got this."

As I stand up and slip on my overalls and worn leather shoes, Josh grabs my arm and adds, "Don't tell Ma, okay? I'm getting better. I just choked a little today."

"I won't tell her," I promise. After all, the last

thing I want is to have Nurse Mabel visit our home again.

———

On our walk to church, Josh seems a little sprier. "Ma, will you tell us about Grandma and Grandpa Burnes?"

It's the story about Pa's parents that he used to recount to us when we were younger.

Ma agrees. "Okay, but just until we reach the edge of town. I don't want anyone else hearing it."

Ma and I match Josh's slow pace. She ruffles his dark hair and begins. "Your Pa's parents were treasure hunters at heart. Both were raised in New York, and they couldn't wait to find their fortune in the West."

I close my eyes, imagining what living in a city as large as New York would be like.

"First, they went to California, hoping to catch the tail end of the Gold Rush. Paps thought panning for gold was sissy's work, so he stuck to mining. But Gammy, well, she was the one with a nose for business."

Josh coughs, and Ma looks worried. But there is nothing she or I can do.

"Every morning Gammy left Paps at the mine entrance and then hiked high into the hills. One day, she found the jackpot—a stream with nuggets the size of raisins in it. Day after day, she worked the stream and brought home tiny sacks filled with golden pebbles. She kept it a secret from everyone, even Paps."

I could just see the two of them—my grandfather, who thought he was the man of the house, working long miserable hours for a pinch of gold dust. All the while, my grandmother amassed a fortune.

"Gammy's plan," continued Ma, "was to get enough money to buy a home and surprise her husband with it. But plans changed when she got pregnant with your father. She became ill and couldn't climb the mountain. She showed Paps the gold and told him about her stream. He was so excited, he went out, got drunk, and spilled the beans to other men at the mine. Within hours, Mama's stream was a madhouse of gold seekers. Even the gold she stored in their house was stolen."

"He was a fool," I say.

"Well," responds Ma, "that all depends on how you look at it. If Gammy had gotten her wish and they'd built a house in California, they might have never found Docketville, and your father would have never found me. Nothing is all bad or good. Just somewhere in the middle."

"Tell us the rest of the story." Josh tries to hold down a small cough, but it escapes.

"All right," says Ma, "it's about done anyway. After Gammy had your father, Paps kept working in the mines, but it wasn't bringing home much money. Gammy decided what she really wanted was to find treasure someone else had already dug from the earth. She learned about gold treasure in Arizona brought here from Mexico by the Aztecs long before America even was."

Josh yawns. Ma sees it and slides her hand

into his. "Gammy even paid money for a map. It showed a rock on top of a mountain in the shape of a turtle's head that marked the spot. You had to look through the eye of the turtle to see where the treasure was buried."

"So, they came here, discovered Turtle Head Rock, but never found the treasure," I say matter-of-factly, finishing the tale quickly.

Josh glares at me, and I shrug. My patience isn't like his.

"That's right," says Ma. "Your grandparents got lost in the wilderness and nearly died from starvation and thirst until they happened upon Docket Senior and his newfound town. He took them in and showed them kindness. They swapped their treasure hunting ways for a life of simplicity."

"And Docket Senior is Preacher Docket's papa?" Josh asks.

"That's right," Ma answers.

"And have you ever looked for Gammy's treasure?"

Ma laughs. "Heavens, no. It's a bunch of nonsense."

But I don't think so. I love to look for Aztec gold in the hills. And just because I haven't found it yet doesn't mean it isn't there.

———

In the chapel, Ruth sits at the very back of the congregational hall. What's left of her hair is pulled into a messy sort of bun. Stray hairs poke out around it. Even so, she puts all of the other girls to shame with her good looks.

My brother elbows me in the ribs, and I follow him up the aisle. We sit in the same row our family has sat on since I was born. From the looks of it, everybody in town is there, making three hundred or more, give or take any new babies being born. I hang my head and do my best to melt into the bench. Gossip echoes around me, and not just from the women. I bite my tongue to stay quiet. Getting angry would only show everyone just how full of iniquity I really am.

"Dear brothers and sisters of the faith," says Preacher Docket. His straight, rigid form looms over us from the pulpit. "Let us bow our heads for the invocation."

Mine's already as low as it can get, but I close my eyes tight and pray as hard as I can for Josh, Ruth, and Ma. I quit praying for Pa's soul a while ago. Now that he's in heaven I figure he should be all right.

Preacher Docket rambles on about shunning the evil among us, serving our neighbors, and giving all of our earthly possessions to the church. At last, he finishes.

"Amen," we repeat and raise our heads.

The building bursts with song. Mrs. Hopkins, our chorister, sways back and forth to the opening hymn. She peers at the congregation, checking which of the young folk are slacking in their "vocal participation" as she calls it. Her eyes land on me and her white baton drops to the floor. She stops the song after only one verse and bustles to her pew near the front. She whispers to her husband, a big burly man, and he turns around, searching the crowd. He finds what he's looking for when our eyes meet. He shakes his head in disgust, and I pray once again. This time for an early death.

Josh pokes me in the leg. I return the gesture, but harder.

"Stop frowning," he whispers. "Ma said you should look as cheerful as possible."

"Easy for you to say," I snarl back at him. "You're not the one who's been marked as the community miscreant."

"True," he answers, "but I am his brother."

His words sting. After all those Sunday School lessons about not bringing shame to my family name, I'd done it anyway.

Preacher Docket is talking again. The man hardly ever stops.

"To have all things in common is godly," he purrs. "'Tis evil to put one above another. For one man to stand in want while others have excess is the lowest form of selfishness. When my father founded Docketville many years ago, he taught the law of equality and how to have no poor among us."

The congregation stirs at the mention of Preacher Docket's father. He died only a month ago.

"Sadly, however, there still is sin among us, wolves dressed in sheep's clothing. Some have gone astray despite the preaching of the good word." He doesn't need to say my name for everyone to know who he's talking about. "Do all you can to guard your children against the influence of evil. We must stay clear of lust. We must remain pure for the approaching Armageddon."

A sob rises in the back. It's Mrs. Ivins, Ruth's mom. Her husband tries to console her, but she's not calming down. Ruth sits next to her father, her jaw set in stone. She glances in my direction, her gaze steady as a hawk's. Again, I wish I'd never been in the stables yesterday, but then I remember feeling her breath on my neck, and I'm not so sure I would have missed that for Armageddon itself.

"If any of you fine mothers of Docketville ever question your responsibility to live a pious life, let us remember how a fallen woman leaves a legacy of deviltry on her children," continues Preacher Docket.

Josh's fists clench, and I worry he's going to start spitting teeth at the pulpit. "What's deviltry?" His body shivers like it's a cold winter morning.

"I'm not sure," I whisper back, "but get a hold of yourself. We don't need more than one evil-doer in this family. I'm going to make things better, promise." I hear a rattle in Josh's chest from his heavy breathing. I've got to do something, or he might start coughing and making a scene. That's the last thing our pitiful family needs today. Without thinking, I'm on my feet, hands outstretched.

"I'm a sinner." My voice rises to the ceiling but stops short of heaven. I can't fool God, but I sure hope I can pull the wool over Preacher Docket's eyes. "I've done wrong in the sight of my fellow brother and sisters, and I'm here to seek forgiveness."

The church hums like a beehive. Mothers, fathers, children, neighbors—they all converse with each other discussing my fate. Preacher Docket remains his stoic self, patiently waiting for the noise to die down.

"Very well, Dillan Burnes," he says. "Be seated."

The crowd quiets.

"You have interrupted our services in the name of repentance. For your sake, I hope your confession is real." He stares into my eyes. "Forgiveness is no easy matter. It takes work. It takes punishment. It calls for languishing of the soul. I, for one, am not convinced you have suffered enough."

The murmuring begins again.

"But," he continues, "if you're sincere in your plea for forgiveness, the Lord will make you strong. In the Old Testament, there is a story of two brothers, Jacob and Esau. They fought each other in the very womb of their mother. In life, Jacob prevailed in wit and strength over his brother because he was upright in his repentance." Preacher Docket waits for it to be quiet enough to hear a feather fall to the floor. "Will one of Dillan's brothers in the gospel fight him in an act of rectitude? If Dillan wins, we know he is forgiven in the eyes of the Almighty. If he loses, we know his penance is not complete."

A commotion in the back of the hall tells me there is indeed someone willing to fight me. I don't need to guess who. Clyde Hampton's hand is raised high in the air. "Preacher Docket," he calls out with excitement, "I volunteer to fight Dillan."

The audience snickers. I might be tall, but Clyde is thick. Full of muscle and spite. He's always been sweet on Ruth, but she's never cared much for him.

"Excellent," answers Preacher Docket. "If Dillan loses, it's a sign heaven does not approve of his repentance. He will have to perform Clyde's community chore as well as his own for one month to learn humility."

My legs are numb. Clyde is a fence builder. He lifts two-foot-wide tree trunks the length of a wagon all on his own. If God is trying to tell me something, I'm hearing it loud and clear.

"You can whip him," Josh says to me as I unbutton my white Sunday shirt. We're on the lawn in front of the chapel. Like me, Clyde strips down to his undershirt and trousers. Even though he's only a year older than me, a few strands of black, curly hair poke out from the neckline of his undershirt. Discouraged, I look at the top of my chest—smooth as a baby's bottom.

"Quit your lying," I say under my breath. "Don't you know it's a sin? Clyde's as solid as a draft horse."

"He might be solid, but he's slow." Josh coughs. "You forget that while he's been building fences, you've been hauling buckets of slop, manhandling swine the size of ponies, and carrying bales of hay. You don't look so bad."

Speaking of pigs, I'm sweating like one right now. I don't know if it's from being in my skivvies in front of Ruth and the rest of the women or if it's because I'm doomed. Maybe both.

"Don't try to duck," continues Josh. "You're too tall. Move to the left and then give him an uppercut with your right arm. It's your strongest."

"Who taught you about fighting?"

Josh puffs out his chest. "Pa."

"He did?" I ask, surprised.

Josh nods. "Last year, when the older boys were bullying us younger ones. He taught me a few things, but he told me only to use them when necessary."

That was Pa for you—built like an ox but as gentle as a lamb.

Preacher Docket calls the crowd to order.

"Brothers and sisters, while it's not Christian to fight for an unholy cause, even Jesus used force to cleanse the temple of Jerusalem. In a similar fashion, let us cleanse Docketville of sin. The fight stops when either of these young men claims surrender." He looks me in the eye. "Understand?"

I do. Part of me wants to give up now, but Ruth is standing front row and center. I still have some pride left in me. In the end, I'm sure that will be my downfall.

"Begin!"

Josh was right. I'm too tall to duck. Clyde's

fist rips through the air. I scrunch my shoulders thinking it will help. Instead, it gives him a clear shot at my jaw.

WHAM.

Pain.

And a lot of it.

The good thing is that Clyde's punch makes me angry. A really unrighteous kind of anger, like when I want to shoot a fox that just sneaked off with some of our chickens in the night.

"Dillan, remember what I said!" Josh hollers.

The next hit comes from the right. I dodge to the left and strike. My knuckles connect with his temple. His skin splits and bright red liquid oozes out.

I drop my hand in shock. I've never hurt anyone before. Clyde sees me let my guard down and slugs me in the gut. I double over. He rams me with his shoulder, and I fall to the ground. Dirt gets into my eyes, and sharp pebbles dig into my chest. I roll over to find Clyde straddling me. He tries to pin my arms to my side with his knees, but I pull them away and connect a fist with his face.

Josh cheers for me. The poor kid never gives up.

Clyde shakes off the hit and begins to pummel me, back and forth, one cheek and then the other.

I hear Ma. I'm amazed her soft voice carries through the shrieks of the crowd. "Dillan. You can do this."

That's it. That's all she says, but it's enough. I slide my hands in between Clyde's arms and fling them to his side. Next, I turn over, slide my knees beneath me, and get on all fours. Clyde, who's on my back, looks like he's a bull rider. I buck him off, and it's his turn to eat dirt.

He leaps up and we clasp arms, like two bucks in an antler lock. I practically lift him off the ground and let go. When he falls, I hit him square in the nose. Blood gushes out and he crawls back in shock.

Like a vulture, I move forward.

One after the next, my swings connect with his jaw. I stop a second, waiting for him to say he's done, but he only grunts, like something is jumbled in his brain. I throw another punch just as Ma yells, "Someone help me!"

I turn to see my brother lying on the ground, twitching like the devil himself is tickling his soul. His eyes are rolled back into his head and spit hangs from his mouth.

I lunge toward him but don't make it there. A force on my back plunges me to the ground. Clyde is above me, kicking my head.

"Stop!" I scream. "Stop! I surrender!"

Preacher Docket's voice booms from above. "The fight is over." He stands next to Clyde, patting him on his shoulder that is covered with blood dripping from his nose. He raises Clyde's hand to heaven. "You have shown the strength of a righteous man." Then, looking down at me, Preacher Docket says, "Let this be a lesson to you, Dillan. Forgiveness is not a matter to be trifled with. Come next time with a humbler spirit, and I shall reconsider."

I only hear half of what Preacher Docket says. Crawling to where my brother is on the ground, I cradle his head in my arms. Ma reaches down and holds his legs. Josh's arms flail, hitting me in the face, but I feel nothing.

I watch helplessly as Josh's body continues to be thrown back and forth by an invisible enemy. At least his coughing has stopped. Out of the corner of my eye, I see Preacher Docket walking about the crowd, handing out licorice sticks to the young like he does every Sunday as if nothing out of the ordinary is happening. The sound of the children thanking him makes my insides burn.

My brother groans and I hold him even tighter. I only want the madness to stop.

At last, it does.

Wiping the spittle from his mouth with my bruised hand, I see most of the townsfolk have turned their faces—in disgust I suppose; a few stare with gaping mouths. One person, however, has tears in her eyes.

Ruth.

4. NO FRATERNIZING WITH STRANGERS

JOSH, with eyes half open, slumps on a stool in Nurse Mabel's home. With its crystal chandelier in the living room and wall-to-wall carpet, it's the nicest house in town. I guess that's a benefit of being Preacher Docket's righthand man—or woman. Ma stands behind Josh, keeping him upright and rubbing his shoulders. Nurse Mabel taps Josh's knee with a tiny hammer. His leg moves a bit, but he can hardly keep himself from falling asleep. She clicks her tongue in disapproval.

"I don't know what happened," Josh mumbles, his face white as a turnip. "I just got this strange feeling that everything around me was moving real slow like. The next thing I remember Dillan was holding me in his lap like a day-old pup." He looks me in the eye. "That was very embarrassing, by the way."

I grin. Leave it to my brother to make a joke.

"You've got a fever," says Nurse Mabel,

mostly to herself, "and of course your lungs rattle like a loose wagon wheel, but other than that, I see nothing wrong. Just a weak constitution, I'm guessing. In any case, you're plenty strong to keep working your family's chore."

What Nurse Mabel doesn't know is that Josh hasn't slopped the pigs for weeks. His body can't take the load, so I cover for him. Nobody notices since the last place townsfolk lollygag is by the pens. Most don't like the stench, though I don't mind it.

"Is it the same thing his father had?" My mom's face is pinched. She hates talking about Pa.

"I don't think so." Nurse Mabel puts down her stethoscope. "Your husband's disease came on fast and furious. All your son needs is to eat more fruit and get lots of fresh air." Nurse Mabel packs her medical tools into a black bag. "In fact," she turns to Ma, "I suggest your boy drinks ten large cups of apricot nectar a day. I'll send the order to the co-op so you can get an extra allotment."

"Apricot nectar?" questions Ma.

"Yes. And for the coughing, I suggest snail syrup." Nurse Mabel rummages about in a cupboard. "Here it is," she announces. "Dillan, copy down the recipe on this paper."

I do as I'm told.

"First," she begins, "collect a bucket full of garden snails. You have to get them early in the morning when the dew is still out. Pull off their shells, slit the bodies, and mix them with a half a pound of sugar."

My hand, bruised from the fight with Clyde, shakes as I write down the instructions. Nurse Mabel is out of her mind. *Snail syrup?*

"Next, put the whole concoction in a bag—cheesecloth is best—and hang it in the cellar with a bowl underneath to catch the drippings." She looks up from her paper. "Snail syrup will take care of his coughing spells. Probably toughen him up as well. He could use it." She talks about Josh as if he isn't sitting less than three feet from her.

Apparently, Ma has heard enough. "Thank you, Nurse Mabel," she says, scooping up Josh in her arms. I follow her out the door, letting the screen door bang behind me.

———

"The woman is a raving lunatic," I say. It's been a week since Josh saw Nurse Mabel, and he's doing worse. Lots worse. He can hardly keep anything down. I think it's the apricot nectar.

"Please, Ma," says Josh, "don't make me drink anymore." His face looks pitiful, like a baby robin that can't find its worm.

"All right," says Ma, "you don't have to drink anymore." She sets down the glass full of thick, orange goo on the table. "I'll send the box of apricots back to the co-op. There's got to be others who would like a little fresh fruit. Dillan, go get the wheelbarrow."

"Can I go with him?" pleads Josh. "Nurse Mabel said I need fresh air."

Ma sighs, knowing she's about to lose this

battle. She never can say no to Josh. "Fine. But, Dillan—"

"I know," I interrupt. "I'll take good care of him."

The evening air brings a little color back to Josh's cheeks. I punch him once in the arm and tell him to climb into the wheelbarrow along with the apricots.

"I won't do that," he scowls. "I'm no sissy."

"You'll do as you're told," I say, "or I'll make a batch of snail syrup and make you bathe in the stuff. Now get in."

He does as I tell him to, but not without shooting me a dirty look first. "Sheesh," he murmurs, "you'd think Preacher Docket was my brother or something."

The wind picks up as I push Josh and the left-over apricots down the road. A wagon passes us. Driving is Jake Simmons, the town baker and Ruth's next-door neighbor. He looks at me and quickly turns his head. Guilt sinks into my chest. In a few weeks, my blue skin will be back to normal, but Ruth's hair will take years to grow. I wish to high heaven there was some way for me to tell her I'm sorry.

"Josh," I say slowly, a plan starting in my mind, "you know how the community center is only a couple blocks away from Preacher Dock-et's Hotel and Diner?"

"Yeah," he says, squishing an earwig trying to crawl out of the wooden box holding the fruit.

"Would you be willing to wait by the co-op while I run over to—"

"You're 'bout as thick as a mule." Josh spits

out a stalk of grass. He must be part dog because chewing on grass makes his stomach feel better. Our mutt used to do the same thing.

I stop pushing and set the wheelbarrow down. "You don't even know what I'm going to say."

"I do too," he argues. "You think I don't know that for the last year you've been sneaking over to Docket's Hotel and Diner to catch a glimpse of Ruth every chance you get? I might be younger than you, but I'm twice as smart."

"I haven't been sneaking over there. I have to go there to collect the slop, dunce cap."

"Is that so?" He laughs. "You feed those pigs the freshest slop in the whole world. You don't let the stuff sit for more than five minutes before you're back behind the diner waiting for more."

He's right of course. But who wouldn't wait around by the diner's door if they knew Ruth might be coming out of it? It just doesn't make sense not to. It's been killing me this past week that I haven't gotten to see her at all. Working both Clyde's fence job and mine, I don't get to the diner till past dark.

I hoist the barrow up and plod forward. Josh stops snickering and his face turns serious. "Don't go, Dillan. If Ruth's pa finds you anywhere near her, he's likely to shoot you. Plain and simple."

"He won't," I say. "It's water under the bridge." The expression is one of Ma's favorites. "I'll just fetch the slop, tell Ruth I'm sorry, and I'll be right back."

"Suit yourself," Josh rolls his eyes. "But you'd better watch behind your back all the same."

At the community center, I shove a few apricots into my pocket for later and return the rest to Mrs. Giles who's about to close up shop for the evening. She gives me a funny look. I don't know if it's because my face is blue, because Josh is sitting in the wheelbarrow, or because she rarely has anyone bring back food. Usually, she gets complaints the other direction.

I find my brother a comfortable place to rest against the trunk of a juniper tree and make sure he has a big swig of water before I leave. There's about an hour of daylight left.

"I'm going to run over to the diner now. If I'm not back before the sun touches the top of West Mountain, you get first dibs on tonight's bath water. Deal?"

"All right," he says. "And if you never come back, don't plan on me coming to look for your stinking corpse. Deal?"

"Relax," I say, slapping him on the shoulder, "vultures will take care of my body before it ever starts to stink."

———

Two blocks from the co-op, someone whistles. I peek around the corner, and sure enough, it's Frank.

"How ya been?" he asks.

"I've been better," I answer. "And you?"

He flips the back of my hat up and it falls off. I lean down, pretending to pick it up, but yank his feet out from under him instead. His back end slaps the dirt like a bale of pitched hay.

"Why you little—" He's up before I know what's happening, locking my head under his armpit. It's awful smelly, and it'd be easy to get away, but I stay put, letting him get his turn.

"Glad you haven't turned soft with that pretty blue face of yours."

"Watch it." I break free from his grip and flex my arm. "You don't want to mess with me. I'm a fence builder now. I've muscles where you've only dreamed of having them." It feels good to be talking about nothing. With Frank, life is easier.

The clatter of horse hooves pounding the ground interrupts us. Two of the largest, blackest horses I've ever laid eyes on trot up the street. They're ridden by the shortest men alive. Their shiny cowboy boots barely reach the top of the horses' flanks. Gripping the reins are hands the size of apples.

"It's the midget men," mutters Frank.

Sure enough. George and Arthur Hyde, not more than six feet high with one standing on the others' shoulders, peer at us from atop their full-grown steeds. Looking at them, you'd never believe they're legendary cattle ranchers. They're not from Docketville, of course, but they come by every so often for supplies and to barter. The hotel and diner were built for men like them: ranchers on their way down to Mexico who are willing to pay ten dollars a night for a soft bed with a hot breakfast in the morning.

"Come on." Frank pushes me. "Let's get a closer look."

He doesn't have to tell me twice. We beeline it down the street.

We're not more than ten feet away when the church bells dong. It's seven o'clock. One of the black steeds rears back, spooked. The midget on top slides off the horse's rump and lands on the ground. The whole things make me want to laugh until I realize the horse isn't acting right. Instead of running free, it begins stomping the ground, like ants are crawling up its legs.

Horseshoes hit the ground inches from the little man's head. He rolls to one side, trying to escape the attack, but it only positions him closer the horse's hind legs.

"Calm down," shouts the midget's brother, but his own horse is getting agitated.

I step toward the panicked beast, pulling the apricots out of my pocket. I open both hands to show the horse I mean no harm. "You're going to be just fine," I repeat in a soft voice. I ease toward the animal, whose attention has shifted from the midget to me. Its breathing is quick and shallow. I fake a yawn to show the horse there's nothing exciting going on.

Its legs stop moving, and it cocks its head to one side. Reaching out, I rub the horse's withers slowly, all the while whispering and offering it apricots.

Seconds later, the midget is up from off the ground, holding the horse's reins.

"Thank you, boy," he says, wiping the dust off of his trousers, "I've only had a week with her, and she's a tender one. Spooks like none I've had before. But my, isn't she a beauty?"

I nod. Her fur glistens like midnight. And her teeth, now chewing fruit, are big and white.

"She is," I answer.

The other midget dismounts his own horse, holding it by the reins. "Brother," he says, "I do believe this boy with the blue face just saved you from becoming flatter than one of Edna's hot griddle cakes."

I'd completely forgotten how crazy I looked with my blue skin.

"Thank you," the midget says, shaking my hand and wiping dirt off of his clothing.

Frank steps forward. "I'd be happy to stable those horses and carry your bags to the hotel and diner."

"That'd be kind of you," the little man answers. "My name is Arthur, and this is my brother, George."

As Frank takes off down the street holding both animals by the reins, the midget named George points at me. "What's your story, boy? How'd you end up looking like that?"

Fraternizing with strangers is not proper, but ignoring a direct question is also downright rude. "Born this way," I say with a face as serious as a funeral corpse. "Nobody knows what happened. Figured my ma must have eaten too many blueberries for her own good—or mine."

Arthur's face breaks into a grin. "I thought in Docketville it was illegal to lie." He slaps me on the leg and chuckles. "You've made my day. First, you save my life and then you make me laugh. You are different than the rest of the folks around here."

In Docketville, being different shouldn't be a compliment. We're all about being the same. Having the same clothes. The same food. Even the same thoughts.

"Listen," he says, "I've got a little something for you." Arthur takes a leather coin purse out of the pocket of his jacket and pulls something out. He holds it in his palm for me to see.

It's a gold nugget, bigger than a turkey giblet. I've never owned any gold before, though I've spent plenty of time searching in the hills above town for some.

He drops the nugget into my hand, where it seems to burn my skin. Money transactions are only supposed to go through Preacher Docket.

"It's yours," he says.

"Th...thanks," I stammer, closing my fingers tightly around it.

A little out of breath from my run in with the midget twins, I use the shadows of the buildings to keep out of sight of the few townsfolk still out. The gold nugget feels heavy in my pocket. Heavy and evil.

On Center Street, I pass the church with its whitewashed walls and bell on top. Past it is a makeshift school, including the town barber shop and what was supposed to be the post office—nobody ever finished building it.

The last structure on Center is the nicest of them all: Docket's Hotel and Diner. Two stories tall and painted bright blue, it looks like a piece of the sky fell down and landed right in the middle of town. Instead of the usual wooden shakes on top, its roof is made with black tar shingles. Preacher Docket special ordered them from Phoenix. It took more than a month for them to come, which is downright ridiculous since any good horse team could make it there in a week's time.

A light shines through one of the windows on the top floor—Preacher Docket's room. He used to share it with his father who died not too long back. I figure the light means the preacher is busy getting ready for his sermon in the morning. I breathe easier. I won't be running into him tonight.

The slop buckets, which are dented, rusty old milk pails, hang on a hook Pa nailed to the wall years ago. This evening they're about half full, but with all the dishes still banging inside the diner's kitchen, there's got to be more scraps coming soon. After settling on the ground in the corner of the alleyway between the old unfinished post office and the hotel and diner, I pull out a block of wood and start shaving a few strips off of it.

I always keep my pocketknife with me. Fact is, I carve pretty well. Mostly I make the easy stuff like horses and bears and that sort of thing. Every once in a while, one sells to a passerby in the diner's gift shop, which means more money for the town to spend on tools or something else we can't make or grow on our own.

I cut off the corners of the block and whittle a good chunk of the fresh-smelling cedar from the top. This will be the head. Before I get to the rest of the body, however, the diner's side door opens and out steps Ruth, dressed in a long, brown skirt and white apron. Her eyes droop and her mouth is turned down, making her look like a basset hound. Not that I'd ever tell her that.

"Psst," I hiss.

She peers into the shadows. I jump up and walk her direction. We lock eyes and she smiles, but it quickly fades.

"Got some slop?" I grin.

"Right here," she answers. She holds a pail of leftovers. I move to take it from her—a gentlemanly thing to do, not to mention that we usually brush hands on the trade. Instead of waiting for me, however, she quickly pours the leftovers into the bucket herself.

"It's the last for the night," she says, turning to go back inside.

"Ruth, wait." I'm desperate. She has to forgive me. "I'm so sorry. I shouldn't have had Frank ask you to go to the barn. It was wrong of me. I deserved to be punished, but you didn't."

Light from the kitchen window reflects off her cheeks. They're wet.

"I should be whipped for a year straight," I continue. "The problem is..." My voice drops. I hadn't thought about this part. What is my problem? Why can't I seem to leave her alone?

She still doesn't say a word.

"Problem is," I begin again but stop. This is the hardest thing I've ever done, including the fist fight with Clyde last Sunday. "Ruth, I like you. I mean really like you. I think 'bout you a lot, probably because you're the most beautiful girl ever. And the nicest too. I don't know what I'll do if you don't forgive me." There, I'd said it straight up, like a man.

"Dillan, it's not your fault." She says it like the call of a morning wren that promises the sun is coming. But then something in her face changes. The sunrise doesn't happen. "But we can't be friends anymore. I'm growing up. I'm going to be a woman in a few years, and I should start thinking about womanly things."

She sounds like her ma, all scowled-faced and irritable.

"Ruth. I'm changing my ways." My voice lowers. "I'm going to become the most pious young man Docketville has ever produced. I'll keep all the Rules. Preacher Docket will see. I'll win him over. But I always want to be your friend, maybe even more someday—"

"Stop." Ruth shakes her head. "Stop talking right now because that's never going to happen."

"You don't know that," I argue. "We've got lots of time. I can prove myself—"

"I'm promised to be married."

Her words flow like poison through my veins. "What?"

"Promised. You know, spoken for."

"But," I stammer, my mouth feeling numb like the rest of me, "you're only fourteen. You've got two years before most girls get engaged and—"

For the second time in less than a minute she interrupts me. "I'm marrying Clyde Hampton. It won't be until I'm sixteen, but my ma and pa have the whole deal worked out with Preacher Docket. It's God's will."

That was nonsense. A lie as false as any fool's gold. This wasn't about God. This was about Preacher Docket punishing me. Everyone knows Ruth and I had been sweet on each other since forever.

But what is Preacher Docket punishing me for? The kiss in the barn? Wasn't the blue face enough? Others my age had been caught kissing, and none of them had received such awful consequences.

Suddenly, the weathervane on top of the hotel and diner whips around from a strong eastern wind. Dirt blows into my eyes. They water, but not from the grit.

I set down the slop bucket and get as close to Ruth as I'm properly allowed. I've got to make her see none of this is right. Preacher Docket will forgive me. He has to.

"I'll talk to Preacher Docket and see if—"

"Ruth, what's taking you so long?" her mother yells from inside. "We've got a mess of silverware to varnish."

"The Lord will take care of me," says Ruth as she grabs my elbow like it's the last sturdy thing on Earth. She squeezes it.

My heart feels as empty as last year's canning jars.

Inside the kitchen, something drops to the floor. "Ruth!" Her mother voice is angry. "Where are you?"

"I've got to go." Ruth darts inside and leaves

me standing all alone, hatred ripping at my soul —if I actually have one, that is.

Ruth is promised to Clyde Hampton.

A slow burn eats its way into my gut. My legs take off running before my brain has a chance to stop them. I'm headed out of town toward the setting sun. I imagine myself as a deer, running from a hunter. One minute turns into five. Sweat drips down my temples, and I feel strong. I want to leave my life behind: the pigs, Ruth, and especially Preacher Docket.

There's nothing left for me in Docketville...except for Josh. Thinking his name stops me dead in my tracks. I turn around, swallow my pride, and make my way back toward the co-op to fetch my brother.

I'm no deer. I'm a possum. Always have been, always will be.

As I round the corner to the co-op, I see Mrs. Giles is on the ground by my brother. His legs jerk back and forth. When Mrs. Giles sees me, she calls out, "Help! He's having another fit."

I run to Josh and crouch down beside him. If this fit is anything like the last one, there's nothing much I can do but help him not hurt himself.

I almost forget Mrs. Giles is still at my side until she speaks. "I'm sorry this is happening to you folks. You're good people and don't deserve it. Your ma was strong to stand up to Preacher Docket. Even married women in town haven't been that brave when he makes his advances."

I've got no idea what she's talking about. My face must tell Mrs. Giles as much. Her cheeks flush and she stands up. "I'll go fetch some water. It might help." And then she's gone.

As Josh contorts and slashes his arms into the air, I think of nothing else but how I'm going to make him better. I think about praying for help, but that would mean I believe someone is there. And right about now, I'm just not sure.

5. NO PILFERING

JOSH LIES STILL on the ground. I'm afraid he might be dead till I see his chest move up and down.

"Josh." I shake his shoulders roughly.

His eyes open along with his mouth. "Dillan," he whimpers, "I don't feel good."

Mrs. Giles is back. She hands me a canteen.

I thank her and lift Josh's head, slowly pouring a bit of the clear liquid in his mouth. He gags on the water but then gulps it down. Some falls off the side of his mouth like he's drooling. I wipe it with my sleeve before Mrs. Giles can see.

At last, he rests his head back on the dirt. "My legs feel funny. They're tingling like when I sit in one spot fishing too long."

I rub his calves back and forth in my hands. "Can you feel that?" I ask.

"Yeah," he answers. "Just give me a minute. I'll be up, good as new."

"I'm taking you to Nurse Mabel." I never

thought I'd ever say it, but what am I supposed to do? Josh is sick and the witch doctor is all we got. I gear up for a fight from Josh, but none comes.

"If you think it's best." His eyes close, and I wonder if he's sleeping, but then I hear him mumbling a prayer. For the first time in my life, I don't join in.

———

"This is a sickness of the soul," announces Nurse Mabel, who is dressed in a plaid flannel robe and nightcap. We're in her plush living room once again. My brother coughs so loudly you'd think he's choking on a whole chicken, feathers, bones, and all. She wags a finger at him. "You've let your faith weaken. These fits are the work of the devil."

Josh can't defend himself. He's too busy spitting up blood into his cotton hanky.

"What are you saying?" I jump up from the three-legged stool I'm sitting on. "You mean he's possessed?"

Nurse Mabel rubs her eyes and begins shoving items back into her black medicine bag. "I believe an evil spirit has taken hold of his body. There's nothing much I can do for him this time of night." A yawn takes over the nurse's face, leaving me with a clear view of her rotten teeth.

"My brother is sick, not possessed." I surprise myself with how strong I sound. "He needs help. He can't sleep from all the coughing. He has no appetite. And thanks to your apricot nectar, he hasn't kept food down all week. He's as skinny as a corn stalk."

She looks up and scowls. She's never jovial and getting her out of bed this evening hasn't improved her less-than cheery disposition.

"You've got to have some medicine to stop his coughing," I say. "I know you fixed up the Johnsons last winter when they were sick."

Retying the strings of her sleep bonnet under her ample neck, she snorts. "The Johnson boys weren't falling to the earth every other day wrestling with the likes of Satan. They just had a case of the croup, that's all. But your brother..." She yawns again.

Glass bottles clank together as she shuts the drawer of her medicine cabinet. Her living room is one of the few in town with carpet, and Josh looks at the floor longingly like he'd like to lie down on it and take a nap. The shades are drawn tight, making the room extra dark. Doilies on the hall table look like spider webs, and yellowed photographs of men and women with serious faces hang on one wall.

"Please," I beg. "Please, Nurse Mabel. Josh is a good boy. Isn't there something you can give him?"

Her mouth purses into a thin line. "Very well, Dillan," she says, "I'll run to the kitchen and fetch you a head of garlic. When Josh's coughing gets bad, have him peel a clove and suck on it. Who knows? It might rid him of any lingering ungodly visitors as well." She shuffles out of the room.

I lunge for her medicine cabinet and scour the labels on the bottles, looking for something that says it's for coughs. Josh's eyes open to the size of chicken eggs.

In a far corner of the cabinet, next to a brown jar marked with skulls and crossbones, is a bottle with the words "For the Curing of Chronic Coughs" across the front. As smooth as butter, I slide the container into my front pocket and pull out a hanky.

Maybe I'm dead inside, but I feel no guilt.

"That's pilfering," whispers Josh, and I give him a look that shuts him up fast. Just then, Nurse Mabel re-enters the room and shoots me an evil eye. I hold up the handkerchief. "There you go, Josh. Here's a clean hanky."

"Time for you boys to leave." She glowers and waves her hands as if swatting a fly. "I'll let Preacher Docket know of Josh's condition. He has remedies for ailments of the spirit."

"I'm sure he does," I mutter and walk to the door with Josh leaning on me. It's not till we're halfway home that I realize she never gave us the garlic. It doesn't matter. I pat my pocket, making sure the glass bottle is still there.

6. NO HUNTING ON THE SABBATH

IT'S the first night in weeks that Josh sleeps for more than a few hours. In the morning, there's a spark of color in his face, which makes Ma and I feel downright chipper. I don't tell her about the medicine, and I make Josh promise it's our secret. No exceptions.

With Josh doing a little better, I get my jobs done early. We do our house chores no matter if it's Sunday or not. Once through, I hightail it for the community barn to meet Frank where I hope to prep the midgets' horses. They didn't ask for our help, but Frank and I hope if we do, they might give us another gold nugget.

On my walk, the air is warm and still, about right for a June morning in Arizona. It's hard to believe that just yesterday I learned about Ruth being spoken for. It feels like forever. Maybe that's because somewhere deep down I always knew I'd never get someone like her. No, Preacher Docket will give me someone like Patsy

Burnam, what with her buck teeth and greasy hair. Even worse, I hear her cooking is as nasty as nasty gets. Even then, I'd eat burnt toast for every meal if I was married to Ruth.

I meet Frank outside the barn. He chews on a long stalk of grass, trying to stay out of the sun so his white skin doesn't burn. We slip inside the wooden building and see the tall steeds in their stalls, chewing on oats. Their black coats shimmer in the light that slips through the barn's small window. The memory of being close to Ruth in this very place tempts my mind down a path it shouldn't go, but then I cringe thinking of her silky hair lying limp on the floor, mixing with the straw and dirt.

"Come on," says Frank. "Let's clean out their shoes."

He reaches out and slides the metal rod that holds the door shut to the side. Before either of us know what is happening, Frank's head and shoulders are covered in manure.

"What the—?" Frank hollers.

I jump back, dodging the brown, stinky clumps that my friend is shaking off his body like a wet dog.

"Where did this come from?" Frank pulls some of the muck out of his hair.

I look up to see a bucking hanging from the rafters. It's turned upside down. A few globs of sticky manure still cling to the rim.

"From up there." I point.

Frank tries to lift his head, but brown liquid dribbles dangerous close to his mouth and he begins to gag.

From behind I hear a low chuckle.

Spinning around, I see George holding his small middle in mid laugh. He takes a breath and asks, "What are you boys doing getting into our horses' stall? I didn't get you two as thieves."

"No!" I say, shocked. "We're not here to steal anything. We came to clean your horses' shoes and get them ready for your ride today."

"That's mighty nice. What made you decide to do that?"

As Frank attempt to clean himself off, I explain. "We thought you might appreciate help."

George waits for me to continue.

"And...we sort of hoped to get another of those gold nuggets."

"Enterprising young men. I like that. But I'm afraid I don't have any more gold to offer you. Not today, anyway. And from the looks of it, your friend needs a bath about now."

"Was that you?" I point upward. "The bucket?"

"Yes. Sometimes people think because we're small we're easy prey. But what we lack in height, we make up for in ingenuity."

"But how?" I ask, amazed.

"Thread. If you're not looking for it, you never see. Your friend tripped our thread trap when he slid the door to the stall open. Consequently, he was the unfortunate receiver of one of our 'safety features', shall I call it? At least this one was benign. On another day he could have ended up with an arrow through his skull."

George doesn't crack a smile and I can't tell if he's pulling my leg or not.

"Next time, we'll be sure to ask first," I say, still keeping my distance from Frank.

"You've got a deal," says George, who turns ready to leave.

"Sir," I call out.

He turns back to me. "Yes?"

I'm afraid to ask but thinking of my sick brother urges me on. "Do you know if the nugget you gave me yesterday is enough for a doctor in Phoenix to take a look at my brother?"

"Well," drawls George, "I'm not sure. I've never had much use for a doctor. Edna cures anything that comes my way."

I'm about to ask who Edna is when Frank gags again and then tells me through gritted teeth it's time to go.

"Thanks, anyway," I say.

As Frank and I walk back to his house, I remember conversations I had with Pa before he died. He'd told me there was a well-used deer trail he knew that could take a person most of the way to Phoenix, but I don't remember where he said the trailhead started.

Frank interrupts my thoughts. "Church is starting soon. I can't go like this."

"Perfect," I say. "I'm not going today either."

Frank stares at me like I'm the ghost of his dead grandpa. "Why aren't you going? Skipping is against the Rules."

"That's right," I answer.

"What are you gonna do instead?" he asks.

I shrug.

"You're really missing church, on purpose?"

His face twists in disbelief with a hint of jealousy. "You've got guts."

"Come with me," I tempt. "It's just one Sunday. We deserve a break."

Franks looks down at his nasty shirt. "Okay," he says, "just let me get cleaned up."

———————

Frank stands at my side, canteen around his neck, bow slung over his shoulder, a quiver of arrows and a knapsack on his back. His bangs are wet and stick to his forehead. My shirt clings to me. I wish I had more water.

"You seem to be looking for something," Frank says. "What is it?"

"Just a little exploring." Truth is, I'm looking for the trail to Phoenix Pa used to talk about. And gold. I'm always looking for Gammy's Aztec treasure.

For practice, Frank and I take a few shots with our muskets at birds flying by. Then we make our way to Turtle Head Rock. The head is the size of a wagon, and the turtle's eye, which is bored through the stone, is the size of a melon. You can look through it like you would a small window. The portion of the shell that touches the turtle's head is covered with ornate arrows that all point the same direction—to the east. I imagine what kinds of tools the people who carved the rock must have used and how it must have looked when it was done, before years of weathering masked its beauty.

As always, Frank and I position ourselves on

the west side of the head and peer through the eye hole to the east, the direction of the arrows. Smack dab in the middle of the hole we see an outcropping of rocks on Longhorn Mountain. The same rocks that have been there ever since I first looked through the turtle's eye. The same rocks that have no treasure buried underneath them. None at all.

Frank takes a swig of water. Something in the bushes rattles. An animal of some kind. A deer maybe. Hopefully not a cougar.

"Shhh," I say to Frank and point to a grouping of trees behind us to our left. This time of year, the leaves are full, making it a perfect place for an animal to stalk its prey.

Frank nods. He hears it too. I rest my hand on the handle of my Bowie knife. I sharpened it last week until its blade shone brightly in the sunlight.

If we weren't thirteen-year-old boys longing to prove our manhood, we would walk on, ignoring whatever is rustling the branches. As it is, Frank holds up his finger and circles it around in the air, telling me to get behind the animal and flush it out. He'll get a better shot. Carefully, he pulls an arrow from his pack.

I creep on the tips of my toes. That's what growing up in the wild teaches a boy: how to hunt as good as any animal. If we bring home a gutted deer, we'll have to take it to my house. Dragging the body through town on a Sunday would cause a ruckus.

Frank loads his arrow, pulls the string back, and waits. With a knife in one hand, I cup the other around my mouth and howl as wolf-like as I know how.

No animal comes darting out of the bush. It's quieter than a church during prayer. That means one thing—it's not a deer. Deer are too stupid to know how to play dead.

I inch backward, hoping not to see the yellow blur of cougar fur, when I spot something blue—most definitely not an animal.

I signal to Frank to lower his arrow, but his eyes are locked onto the hiding target, and he doesn't see me. One tiny move from whatever is in those trees, and it's dead. Frank's a crack shot.

I bend down to get a better look. Human eyes lock hold of mine. My heart drops.

"It's Josh!" I yell as Frank releases his arrow into the trees.

7. NO LOITERING AFTER DARK

I CRAWL over the low-lying weeds to where I'm sure my dead brother's body lies. Instead, Josh bolts from the shrubbery, his face sheet-white.

"What are you doing?" he yells. "Trying to kill me?"

He's alive. I stand and rush toward him, grabbing his shoulders and slapping him on the back.

"Now I know you're trying to do me in," he wheezes.

"You gave us a scare," says Frank, running up to us. "I thought I shot you for sure."

Josh turns. An arrow is stuck, dead center, through his bedroll. We drop to the ground in laughter. Josh turns to coughing, which quiets Frank and me.

"Josh," I say, "what are you doing here, and why did you bring all that stuff with you?"

Sheepishly he answers, "I thought you guys

were skipping town. I didn't want to get left behind."

"We're not skipping town." My face flushes.

"Nah," adds Frank, "your brother just dragged me out here to go exploring." He rolls his eyes. "You might as well come along too."

"Great." Josh's face lights up.

I eye him carefully. "Are you sure you're up to it?"

"I am. Besides, Ma's at church. She won't know I'm gone."

For fun, we head over to Longhorn Mountain, the place where the eye of Turtle Rocks says the treasure should be. We climb over boulders, move bushes, and push aside rocks—anything we can think of to find a cave, a marker, or a clue. We've done it all before. As expected, we come up empty-handed. We sit down on the ground and pull out a very late lunch: boiled eggs, a slab of dried beef, and fresh peas from the garden. We drink the last of our water, except for a swig that I plan on making Josh drink later. His throat gets so raw from all the coughing.

With full bellies, we can't fight the urge to take a rest in the shade. When I wake up, I see the sun is only a sliver behind the western mountains. "Guys, we're late. We've got to get home."

If we hurry, we'll make it to the foothills by late evening, and then we'll have to pick our way home in the dark.

I jump up. Frank and Josh are on their feet in seconds, but my plan to hurry doesn't work. It doesn't take long for Josh's raspy breathing to fill the evening quiet of the mountains.

"Drink this," I say, handing him the last swallow of water. "It's an order."

"I'm fine," Josh protests.

I won't hear of it. "Now!"

"All right." He gulps down what's left and catches his breath.

Before long, the sun gives up its last rays, but the foothills are still well below. Frank is getting fidgety, and to be honest so am I. "Should we stop and wait for the moon to come out?" I suggest. "Might make the hiking go easier."

"I've got to get home," answers Frank. "My parents are going to be worried sick as it is."

I think of Ma pacing the living room floor, wondering what has happened to her boys, and my stomach tightens.

"You've got a point," I say. "Let's keep moving." The sun is gone now, and blackness surrounds us. The only way we're getting home tonight is if the good Lord is on our side, which I'm sure he's not. Not even Josh's pureness can make up for my sinner's soul.

After another ten minutes of stumbling in the dark, and I'm completely lost. But since I'm the leader, I keep pretending. At last, Frank calls my bluff.

"You don't know where in tarnations we are, do you?"

"Nope," I admit. "Do you?"

"No," he says, disgusted. "But I'm sure it isn't this way. I say we skirt to the left."

"It's your call," I say. Josh and I fall back and let Frank forge the trail. It feels like we're making progress, at least a little bit, until Frank pulls to a quick stop. Josh runs into his back.

"Holy   fiddlesticks,"   Frank   says.   "Don't move."

"What?" I ask.

"There's nothing in front of me."

I rip the sack off of my back, pull out some matches, and light one. The flame immediately is blown out by a pesky wind. I light another, and this time I shield it with my body. The small circle of light glows like a needle in a haystack of black hay. I lean forward, into the open air, and see dark shadows below.

"You're right," I say. "But I'm thinking the canyon must drop in just below us, probably six feet or so. If we can get down there, we're home free."

"And just how do you think you're going to do that?" Frank asks, backing away from the edge.

"With Josh," I answer. "We'll lower him as far as we can over the cliff's edge." I turn to my brother. "Are you game?"

"Sure," he says, no hesitation.

"When your foot hits the ground," I continue, "we'll know how far it is. Then Frank and I will just jump down." I sound confident, but I'm not so sure on the inside.

"Let's get this over with," Frank says.

I clamp onto Josh's hands, and he scoots backward over the cliff. Soon everything but his elbows on up hangs over the edge.

"I can't feel anything yet," he says, "Drop me lower."

I let him down more. I am on the ground, flush with the cliff's edge, arms hanging over the ledge.

"I think there's something down there," says Josh. "Can't you let me down further?"

I cinch my fingers around his skinny wrists and slide further into the wall of blackness. Frank grabs my legs from behind as Josh begins to swing back and forth, stretching his legs to find purchase.

"I feel something," he calls. "Can you give me another bit?"

The moon's still not up. In the pitch dark, I scoot forward again, hanging my right shoulder inches over the edge. Frank tightens his hold on my legs. Josh's hand is sweating something fierce.

"Josh?" My voice is strained. "Do you feel anything now? Anything at all?"

"Not exactly," he calls back up. "But when I look down it seems like there are shadows of rocks and things. There's got to be something close. Just let go of my hands and I'll land on it."

"Don't be a fool," I say. "I'm bringing you up."

"No," he says. "We're so close. It's like the tips of my boots are grazing the ground. Just drop me."

Hanging on the side of a mountain like that convinces me that praying might not be such a bad idea. I strain my neck to the side, look at the ink-colored sky, but before I can get the first word of a prayer out, Josh's left hand slips out of my grip.

8. NO ANIMALS INDOORS

I DIVE DOWNWARD and claw at my brother's other hand. From behind me, Frank grunts. "You're slipping." He's got me by the boots and that's about it. Taking some of Josh's flesh with me, I regain a firm grip on his wrist.

"Up!" I yell.

Frank pulls. My shirt bunches around my neck, and the rocky soil scrapes my stomach. When I feel my whole body on solid ground, I yank Josh up and he nearly flies over the edge. Safe. Alive. And grumpy.

"What did you do that for?" he asks, rubbing his fresh scratches. "I was fine."

"We're waiting for the moon," I answer. Without another word, I lie on the ground, rest my head on my forearm, close my eyes, and pretend to sleep.

The next thing I know, Frank is shaking me like I'm a baby's rattle. "There's something you gotta to see. We've been walking in circles. We're back on Longhorn Mountain near where we hunt for treasure."

A three-quarter moon gleams in the summer sky, giving form to the bushes and wildflowers. Frank leads me to the place where we hung Josh over the cliff. Frank motions for me to follow him. Flat on our bellies, we ease toward the edge. Below is the canyon floor more than a hundred feet down. Jutting from the side of the cliff, about ten feet from where we're at, is an enormous Cypress tree growing straight out of the rock— our mysterious shadow and what Josh had thought was the ground.

My stomach turns woozy thinking about what would have happened if I'd let go of Josh.

"Whose half-baked idea was it to hang your kid brother over that?" Frank slaps me on the back as we stand up.

Ignoring him, I lift up my eyes to the moon and whatever lies beyond it. "Thanks," I say to the heavens. I might be a sinner, but I'm no ingrate.

Frank and I make a cairn near the spot where we hung Josh by stacking rocks a foot high. We use larger ones on the bottom and smaller rocks up top. It's a warning; no need to tempt death twice. I let Josh sleep another hour before getting him up to start the trek home.

———

Exhausted from yesterday's adventure and Monday's full work schedule, I sit in Ma's rocking chair and wait until it's time for dinner.

The smell of the biscuits and gravy Josh cooks make my stomach feel like a hundred beetles are running around inside of me.

A loud knock ricochets on the front door. I reluctantly get up from the rocking chair to answer it.

"Evening," says Preacher Docket, tipping his top hat my direction. Instantly, Ma appears. I slip next to the wall and slink back into the corner. Being that close to Preacher Docket makes me nervous about all the rule breaking I've been doing lately.

"I'm here to see Joshua," says Preacher Docket, pushing his way inside. "Nurse Mabel sent me. She says his problems are of the spirit, not the body."

"My son's doing just fine," Ma answers, rubbing her dirty hands on her apron.

"Virginia, you know lying is a sin." Preacher Docket straightens the lapels of his black jacket. "Now tell me the truth. Is your boy still filled with unclean spirits that take over his body?"

"He's been coughing less and eating more."

"You know I'm not talking about that," says the preacher.

The odor of burning sausage wafts into the living room. Maybe Josh left it cooking and ran away? A part of me hopes he did. Peeking around the corner, I see him standing by the stove, white as a sheet and not paying a lick of attention to our scorching dinner.

It's not fair. Josh is as nice as nice gets, but nothing good ever happens to him. Once again, I wish I had more than just the one gold nugget I sewed into the waistband of my pants. If I had more, I could make everything better.

The preacher's voice deepens. "I'm on an errand of the Almighty. Step out of my way, woman."

Heeled shoes click across our hardwood floor. Josh's body tenses, and I'm afraid another one of his fits might come on.

"Boy," says Preacher Docket, "leave your woman's work and sit. We're going to find your soul peace this very evening."

Trembling, Josh takes the pan off the stove and walks to the smooth oak chair Pa made for Ma when they were first married. Preacher Docket's voice breaks into a fervent rumble as he begins singing one of his all-time favorites:

> Day of wrath, O day of mourning!
> See fulfilled the prophet's warning,
> Heaven and earth in ashes burning.

He waves his arms back and forth, a sign he wants us to accompany him. Ma and I sing loudly in our best alto voices, but Josh's lips don't move. He's frozen in place.

> Oh, what fear man's bosom rendeth
> When from Heav'n the Judge
>   descendeth
> On Whose sentence all dependeth!

The words echo off our walls. Preacher Docket turns through the pages of his scriptures like a half-starved wolf hunting for its prey.

"There's a story told about a man who lived up in the caves above Jerusalem. He lived away from people because of sin. He was possessed, just like you, Joshua." Preacher Docket smacks his lips together. "Being the kind and compassionate person that Jesus was, he went to see the man. Do you know what happened?"

Josh nods. He knows the story. We all do. It's been retold to us many a time over the pulpit by Preacher Docket himself.

"What did the Lord Jesus do?"

Josh's lungs rattle when he answers. "Jesus commanded the evil spirits to go into a herd of swine, and they did."

"Excellent!" Preacher Docket claps his hands together like he's a schoolboy winning a match of marbles. "Jesus rid the man of Satan's influences just like you and I clean varmints from the cellar."

Silence.

Raising his hand ever so slightly, Preacher Docket points to me. "Swine is the same thing as pigs," he says. "You know that, Dillan?"

"Yes, sir."

"Good," he says. "I didn't see you at church yesterday. I wasn't sure if you'd forgotten the holy writ."

I hold my ground. He'll hear no apology from me.

"Let us pray and see what the Lord would have us do." He begins the prayer, saying every syllable with gusto. He gives thanks for our blessings and asks for help against temptation. He picks up speed when he mentions Josh and the possession by evil spirits. Pleading for inspiration, Preacher Docket stops mid-sentence and moans something fierce. He carries on for a bit and then whispers, "Amen."

Ma and Josh repeat the phrase. I don't.

"The answer has been given to me," the preacher announces. "A sacrifice is needed."

You could have heard a gnat land on the kitchen table. After all, it hasn't been that long since Nurse Mabel used the Gentian Violet to color me blue. My mouth turns as dry as a hundred-year-old well.

"What kind of sacrifice?" Ma asks.

"A pig," the preacher answers. "The biggest pig there is in the community pen." His mouth upturns. "Dillan needs to carry it from town, by himself, to the house. If he can do it before the sun sets, I will be able to rid Joshua's soul of the evil living inside of it."

This isn't an answer to prayer. It's just another way to break me. That's as clear as the smirk on Preacher Docket's face.

One of my jobs is to let the butcher know when it's time to slaughter a pig, which happens right around three hundred pounds. Last week my biggest animal, Samson, weighed in at two hundred and sixty, meaning he's only a few months out from becoming bacon. I know I can lift him onto the butcher scales, but carry him two miles? I clench the muscles in my arms and legs. My fists curl.

Ma shakes his head. "Preacher Docket," she begins. "That seems a little—"

"Ma," I interrupt her, "please fetch me the ropes."

By the time I reach the pen in town only an hour of light is left. First thing I do is feed the pig some rotting fruit. I hope the fermentation will relax Samson and make him easier to carry.

The animal squeals in delight, and its pen mates gather around for a taste. I shoo them away. The last thing I need is an audience. Using one of the ropes, I hogtie Samson's legs without much trouble. Now comes the tricky part. I weave the second, longer rope into a mess of knots, interlinking them, to make a net of sorts. I lie it on the ground, pick up the pig, and set it down on top of the crude net.

Next, using the ends of the rope for leverage, I lift the pig in the air behind me, high enough that I'm able to bend my neck way back and poke my head in between its belly and hoofs. I imagine it must look like Samson is choking me, and I smile at the thought.

Leaning forward, I slide the pig onto my shoulders. Its size is impressive, but the noises it makes are high and pitiful. Nothing likes to be hog-tied. Especially not hogs.

Wrapping the rope around my waist and tying the strongest fisherman's knot known to man, I secure the pig tightly to me even though it's wiggling like an earthworm in the rain. Now all I have to do is walk home. I wonder how long

Preacher Docket has been dreaming up this punishment.

Ignoring the pressure on my back, I walk out of the pen, close the gate, and march forward, counting each step as I go. One, two, three...

. . . Four hundred and twelve, four hundred and thirteen, four hundred and fourteen. I'm numb from my chin to my knees. My feet, on the other hand, feel every pound of the animal I've got strapped to me. My body shakes a little, and I breathe in short spurts. I'm several hundred yards past the town's center, meaning I've got a mile and a half left. Maybe a little more.

At least the fermented fruit is working. Samson has settled into blissful snoring. Even though his body is now easier to carry, it makes me feel more alone than ever. It's just me and my thoughts.

As usual, Ruth comes to mind—the way we used to play kick the can summer nights night, sing Christmas carols in the winter, and bob for apples at the Fall Festival. One year she dunked her head all the way into the water just to beat me. It was in good fun, of course, and I still remember thinking how alive she looked with wet hair and an apple poking out of her mouth. Pa had laughed and told her she looked like a stuffed pig.

Pa.

I don't want to think about him. I push the image out of my mind, refusing to remember his teasing smile that made his eyes shine as bright as a bonfire at night. At least, that's what Ma used to say. She said it was Pa's smile that first melted her heart.

My parents met in 1903 after President Roosevelt announced he would pay wages to anyone who helped build the dam on the Salt River. Docket Senior got the idea to send some of Docketville's strongest men to Phoenix to earn money to build a school in Docketville. Pa went and that's where he'd met Ma.

Pa was nineteen and Ma was too. Plenty old to get married, but Ma's parents didn't like the idea of her leaving them to go into Arizona's southern wilderness. The two had eloped and had me a year later.

A shooting pain down my spine saves me from dredging up any more memories. Flies buzz around my ears and into my nose. I'd like to swat them away, but my fingers are twisted into the ropes and are about as useful as tree stumps. Peering past the sweat drizzling off my forehead, I see the Cowley's farm. It's only a half mile to our farm from here. Their kids are outside, killing grasshoppers with brooms. The youngest sees me and shrieks. His mother runs out the front door to see what is going on. Once she sees me, her eyes open as big as saucers. I must be a sight. But I'm glad they're watching. The part of me that hates to lose wakes up, pouring life back into my arms and legs. I stumble on some loose gravel, catch my balance, and quicken my step. What I would give for a cold glass of water 'bout now.

The sun teases the mountains, reminding me I only have another twenty minutes or so. The thought makes blood pound in my head, and I beg for mercy. The second I'm out of sight of the Cowley's farm, my body hits an invisible wall. I'm lucky I don't fall over backward.

A squeal pierces my ear. Samson's awake, and he isn't happy. I shush him. It works about as well as a square wagon wheel.

More shrill noises come from up top my shoulders. I can't take much more. Between the stabbing pain in my neck, the throbbing in my lower back, and the crushing weight in my chest, I feel I've been mauled by a mountain lion. Make it five mountain lions.

I lost count of my steps a while ago but decide to pick it back up. Two thousand and one. Two thousand and two. Two thousand and three. At two thousand and forty-nine I can't see. My eyes are open, but everything is fuzzy gray. My feet, now easy prey to washed out ruts in the road, cautiously inch onward.

I don't know when my house appeared, but at step two thousand eight hundred and sixty-six, I hear a holler. It's Ma. Her voice tastes like manna. My legs get ahead of me, and I fall face-first into the hard dirt. The pig crushes my head, pinning me to the ground and smothering my mouth. I can't breathe. Panic rises to my throat, and I let loose a muffled scream that blends with Samson's whelps.

A prayer starts in my head: *Oh, have mercy.*

Don't, I tell myself, *don't do that*! This battle is between Preacher Docket and me. God is not invited.

Like a whipped bull, I rear off the ground. Roaring, I bring my legs under my chest, and I force myself up. I lumber toward Ma, legs wobbling. One good thing is that my eyes can see again, even though blood pours into them from a gash above my eyebrow.

Then I do the strangest thing. I start to sing Ma's favorite hymn. Surely, I've gone plumb mad.

"All creatures of our God and King."

Samson snorts, sending spittle into my face.

"Lift up your voice and with us sing."

Ma chimes in.

"Alleluia! Alleluia!"

I'm almost there. I keep singing. The setting sun casts its shadows around me, but I've got time. Power surges through my tormented body. Two thousand nine hundred and seventy-three. Two thousand nine hundred seventy-four.

"Alleluia! Alleluia!"

I lift my chin. Samson knows something is about to happen and he quiets. One foot after another I continue. Two thousand and nine hundred and ninety-three. Ma rushes to me and opens the door to the house. Tears fall from her cheeks. I march inside, pig and all. Two thousand nine hundred and ninety-four. I'm home. My knees buckle, and I crumble into Ma's arms. She pries my fingers from out of the ropes and starts untying the knots.

Samson whinnies and vomits rotten fruit all over the floor. Preacher Docket sits as stoic as ever. But if you ask me, he's hiding a whole flour sack full of disappointment.

"Preacher Docket," I say, "there's your pig."

———

Josh shivers on a chair. His shirt is off, and his white skin glows in the firelight. His bones stick out of his thin skin every which direction. A passerby might mistake him for a skeleton. The pig, still hogtied, snorts at my feet in the living room while the preacher rummages inside his battered briefcase he brought with him. Ma grabs a quilt, wraps it around Josh, and then sits beside me on the bench. Her arm supports my body that can't stop shaking.

"It's time," says Preacher Docket, his face the spitting image of someone who just ate a handful of unripe plums, "to proceed."

My brother pulls the blanket tighter around him.

The preacher pokes at Samson with the tip of his fancy black shoe. "And that," he says, "is a very large pig."

Samson returns the compliment with a grunt and some slobber.

"Joshua, all that is left to do is to command the devil spirit to leave your body and go into the pig's. Then I'll bestow the mark of protection on you. Are you ready?"

A blank stare on Josh's face tells me he doesn't know what Preacher Docket is talking about any more than I do.

"Preacher Docket," says Ma, letting go of me, "what is the mark of protection?"

At that very moment, it dawns on me that Preacher Docket is holding a miniature branding iron with the stamp of a cross on the end. He positions the iron into the crackling fire and rests the handle on the hearth.

"If I am going to cast out a devil out of his body, I certainly am not going to let it go right back in," he answers, turning the rod in his hand. "Josh needs extra protection, seeing how his body is in a weakened state."

Ma's hands wring together, her face angrier than I've ever seen before.

"You're insane!" I cry out. "You're not cursing my pig or branding my brother."

Preacher Docket rises to his feet. So do I.

"Boy, do you know who you're dealing with?" he asks me. Then, turning to Ma, he guffaws. "How the mighty have fallen. My father would be shocked to see what your family has become."

The branding iron takes on a slight red glow.

Preacher Docket continues. "Virginia, I remember when your husband's parents came to Docketville. Starving and homeless. Your late husband looked half dead. A pitiful child. My father took them in, fed them, gave them work, and helped them built you a home. And how did your husband thank him? By raising his sons to be rebellious and ungrateful."

"My husband's family owes a lot to your father—" begins Ma.

Preacher Docket interrupts her. "Who do you think raises the food you eat? Keeps you clothed? Provides you safety? I do!"

Ma stands, resting her hand on my shoulder. "Poindexter Docket," she says to the preacher, "get out of my house. Get out and never come back."

Preacher Docket glares at her. "You will wish you never said that." He picks up his briefcase, stomps to our door, and leaves, but not before I realize I never knew his first name was Poindexter. Laughter spills out of my mouth. I can't help it. Poindexter Docket. Maybe someone in heaven does have a sense of humor.

9. NO PARTIES

MONDAY MORNING COMES TOO SOON for all of us. It was hard falling asleep. Preacher Docket's threat hangs in the house like the stench from a dead mouse in the walls. I wake to Ma's frantic voice. "Dillan!"

I run downstairs. My whole body aches from carrying Samson the day before. But the minute I see Ma's face, I don't think about my sore muscles anymore. I can tell she doesn't have good news.

"He's dead," she says.

I first think of my brother. "Josh?" I whisper, bile rising in my throat.

"No, Samson," Ma answers. "His throat's been slit." She points out the back door.

In the yard, lying on the dirt in a pool of blood, is Samson. I'd left him there for the night until I could get him back to the pen.

"We need to get the body to Floyd. Maybe some of the meat is still salvageable." Ma shakes her head. "A lot of families were planning on him for food this winter."

Ours included.

I heft Samson into the wheelbarrow and take off for the butcher's, barely taking time to change out of my pajamas. My stiff shoulders scream their disapproval, but pain is only for the weak. I pass a few of our neighbors who huddle in hushed circles once they see my cargo. The night was a warm one and the smell of rot has already set in.

In front of the church, the choir practices. Ruth and her parents are there. It hits me that I like Ruth's hair short. Today she's wearing it straight, and it ends right where the smooth of her neck begins. Even though her Sunday dress is simple, she looks like an angel in it. On a normal day, I'd stop and listen. But I don't have the time. The words of the song fade behind me.

> Softly the wings of a dove beat,
> Breathing a message unheard,
> Love with a gentle persuasion
> Whispers her comforting word.

"Get that foul—smelling animal out of here," booms a voice. Clyde Hampton and his father, Dirk, lean against the barber shop's front door with nice clothes, hands in their pockets, hair slicked back. They make quite a sight next to me —dirty, sweating, and hauling a mangled pig to the slaughterhouse.

They saunter forward, a knowing look in their eyes. Clyde looks altogether too clean, too spiffy, and too smug. He's as guilty as a fox in a hen house.

"Did you enjoy killing an overweight, drunk pig last night?" I ask. "Or did your daddy do it?"

Clyde turns to me. "Why you—" He lunges forward. I hadn't planned on it, but instinct kicks in and I dart behind the wheelbarrow, blocking my path with Samson's body. Clyde overcorrects, trips, and lands smack dab on top of the pig's bloody body.

"Pa!" He screams. His father bolts next to him and lifts him out of the mess. His shirt is red, darkened blood clots hang from his chin. Scraping them off, Clyde throws them at me. I don't duck. It's a clear miss.

"You keep your mouth shut and your eyes to yourself," he howls, spit flying from his mouth. "She's mine now. You got that? Ruth will be my wife while you tend to your disgusting little pig pen."

I don't want to talk about that. I don't have the energy. But I hate to let Clyde think he's outsmarted me. "I don't have time to stay and chat about your fairytale dream. This pig needs attention."

——————

People are at work and the streets are empty as I make our way back home. Samson's body was past fresh, but Floyd thought some parts might still be useable for sausage. I'd stayed and helped for a few hours.

As I pass the church, something white on a

low hanging branch of a maple tree catches my eye. I fetch what turns out to be a white hanky folded into the shape of a dove. On one of its wings, embroidered with red floss into the cloth, are the initials: R. I. It's Ruth's hanky, all right, but why did she make a bird out of it? Then the words of the song she'd been singing earlier at the church that morning enter my mind:

> Softly the wings of a dove beat,
> Breathing a message unheard,
> Love with a gentle persuasion
> Whispers her comforting word.

Maybe, just maybe, Ruth doesn't hate me after all.

————

After a long day of fence building and caring for the pigs, the only thing I want to do is drop into bed and fall asleep. When I open the front door to the house, however, the sweet smell of cake hits me full force. Josh sits in Ma's chair snapping off the ends of green beans. Someone has decorated the living room with newspaper streamers and yarn.

"That smells amazing," I say, confused.

The grin on Josh's face grows wide. "Happy birthday, Dillan!"

I'm stunned; I totally had forgotten it was my birthday. Fourteen years ago, I was born. I feel more like fourteen going on one hundred.

Birthdays have always been a big deal to Ma.

She likes to make a special cake and dinner. When I was younger, we'd sing songs, play games, and even give presents. All of that is against the Rules now. God is the only one to give gifts, and those are of the spiritual kind. Earthly gift giving causes one person to have something more than someone else.

In the kitchen, cinnamon and nutmeg overtake me, and I breathe in long and hard.

"Ma wants to know if you'd rather eat inside at the table or outside on a blanket," Josh asks. "You know, like a picnic."

It all feels so strange. Like a dream. Earlier this morning, while dodging pig guts, I would have laughed if someone had told me this day was going to turn out to be a good one. But it had. First, there had been the present from Ruth, then spice cake, and now a picnic. Things are looking up.

"Outside," I answer. "I'll go get the quilt."

———

Resting under the big oak tree with my belly full of good food feels like what I imagine heaven to be. Josh is coughing, but it started from laughing too much, which makes it a better cough. Ma pounds his back and makes a game of it. A steady wind coaxes me to close my eyes and relax, but I fight back, not yet ready for sleep.

I finger the cloth dove that is in the pocket of my overalls. One wing has come undone, and the other is about to follow suit. Nothing good ever lasts. Even today is almost over. Shadows creep over the rocks and ground.

"More cake?" asks Ma.

"I've had enough," I answer. "I'm going to have to roll out of bed in the morning."

Resting on the blanket, Josh whistles. It's the happy birthday song. Preacher Docket calls it a pagan ritual, but that never stopped Ma from teaching it to us.

"Ma," Josh says, a little uncertain, "why do you think God took Pa from us?"

For a moment, Ma pauses from gathering the leftover food. "I don't know," she finally answers. "I really have no idea." She thinks a little longer. "I do know he never felt like he belonged here. Not like his parents did. Maybe dying was his way out."

My ears perk up. "Pa didn't like Docketville?"

"No, that's not true, exactly," answers Ma. "He liked some things about Docketville, and those were the reasons he stayed. But there were some things that didn't feel right to him."

"How about you?" I ask Ma. "Do you like it?"

Abruptly, she stands up. "Time to go inside. It's getting late."

10. NO TALKING PAST MIDNIGHT

LONG INTO THE NIGHT, Josh and I whisper to one another in bed.

"Josh, do you realize I only have a few more years till I'm a man?"

"Hadn't thought about it much." His voice sounds tired, and I feel guilty for not letting him rest.

"But with Pa gone, I've felt like a man now for a while. It's not what I thought it would be. Most of the time it just makes me tired."

"You think you're a man?" Josh grunts.

It feels like old times when we used to tease each other, complain about working too much, and swap secrets long into the night. Pa would reprimand us, reminding us nighttime was for sleeping, not gabbing. Then Ma would tell him to hush up, and we'd keep on talking.

"Yes," I say, "yes I do feel like a man."

Josh turns over in bed. "Don't worry, Dillan," he says. "You'll never be a man to me."

I grab the blanket from off him and threaten to push him out of bed. He pretends to resist, though we both know he couldn't fight off a flea. I then wrap him back up like a caterpillar in a cocoon, tucking him in tightly while he coughs and coughs.

"Go to sleep," I say. "You'll know what I mean when you're older."

"Sometimes I think I might never get older," Josh's voice grows serious. "Sometimes I think I'm following Pa's footsteps."

"Stop it!" I hit the mattress. "Don't you dare talk like that, or I will kick you out of bed."

In the candlelight, I see that Josh's face is serious.

"Dillan," he says, "what would you do if you knew something that no one else knew?" Under the blankets, his hands fidget like an old lady knitting.

"First off, I'd tell my older brother, so he didn't torture the secret out of me."

"But what if it's something so bad you still wouldn't tell?"

"Then I wouldn't bring it up."

I lie back in bed and wait for sleep. Josh tosses and turns for a minute or two and then taps my arm. "Seriously, have you ever known something you really wanted to tell someone?"

"Sure," I answer. If Josh thinks I'm going to beg him to tell me whatever it is that's bugging him, he's wrong. I am, after all, older and smarter than him.

"What's your secret?" Josh asks.

"I tried to kiss Ruth Ivins in the community barn."

Josh laughs. "Why, that's as private as getting your hair cut at the barbershop."

I let out a fake huff. Josh reaches his cold toes over and warms them on my feet.

"All right," I say. "There is something I've never told anyone."

"Really?"

"Yes."

"What is it?"

"Someday," I whisper, "I'm going to find Turtle Head Treasure, leave Docketville, and take you and Ma with me."

"That's not a secret."

"It is too."

"It isn't. And besides, where would we go?"

"Maybe New York," I answer.

Just then a coughing spell takes over Josh's body. I pat his back until his body finally relaxes. Without another word, I blow out the candle and think of the gold nugget sewn into my pants. It will probably be the most money I'll ever have. And sadly, it's not enough.

———————

Aztec crowns and jewels the size of pears haunt my dreams until I wake, as ornery as a skunk. I go about my morning chores like I'm trudging through leftover porridge. Josh does the same. That's what happens when you stay up late talking.

Milking Trudy, our cantankerous cow, is my least favorite job. She has kicked me more times in the head than she has hooves. This morning she's in a bad temper. After giving only half a bucket of milk, she bends her back legs and sets herself in the dirt, challenging me to make her stand up.

But I'm in no mood for it.

Setting the milk in the coolest corner of the barn, I finish collecting the eggs. Tuesday is cheese day, which means I have to take the milk to the community co-op where Mrs. Giles dumps it into a cider press and makes the biggest block of cheese known to man. She'll divide it up among the families later.

Behind the barn, rows of corn stand motionless. With no wind, the day promises to be a hot one. I dread going to build fences. Most of the fellows Clyde works with don't like him any more than I do. However, they fear him, and that means they're following his orders to make my life miserable. I'm always stuck carrying the roughest logs, the kind that give me as many slivers as if I'd rolled through a wild raspberry patch all day.

The co-op bustles with families dropping off harvests and picking up their weekly allotments. I'm excited to see beef jerky and honey in the supplies. Those are Josh's favorite.

"How's your brother faring?" questions Mrs. Giles.

"A little better," I answer, thinking of the cough medicine I stole.

"Good to hear it. He's such a nice boy."

Someone behind me whispers that Josh couldn't be all that nice with a brother like me.

The familiar feeling of being trapped overtakes me. The co-op, the church, the town—all of it makes me as claustrophobic as a rat in a snake hole. What if something inside me snaps and I take off? What would happen to Josh? To Ma? To Ruth?

Thinking Ruth's name calms me. I remember the hanky in my pocket. I need to see her. Thanking Mrs. Giles, I head toward Docket's Hotel and Diner.

———

The bell on the front door rings as I enter. Mr. Ivins pushes down his spectacles and sours his face. "The slop bucket is outside as usual," he says. "No need to come in."

"I've already fed the pigs this morning," I answer. "I'm here to see Ruth."

"Ruth is busy." He didn't use to hate me, but ever since I was caught taking advantage of his daughter he's made it perfectly clear he'd like to throw me to the wolves.

"She lost something, and I need to give it back to her." I stand my ground, using my height to my advantage.

"I'll be sure she gets it." He holds his hand out, anticipating I'll put whatever I have into it. He's wrong.

"No thanks," I respond. "I'll be seeing her in person." It wasn't a question but a statement, and it takes Ruth's father by surprise. He doesn't stop me as I climb the stairs. At this time in the morning, Ruth will be upstairs making the beds for the next set of guests.

I find her in the spare room next to Preacher Docket's room—the one he shared with his father when he was still alive. Ruth's back is to me. She grunts as she lifts the mattress, tucking and folding the corners of the cotton sheets just right. Her short blonde hair swings back and forth, and I toy with the idea of hollering "Boo!" Instead, I clear my throat.

"Dillan?" Her head cocks to one side in surprise. "Everything all right?"

"Not really," I answer. "And you?"

She looks past me, checking for extra ears, then grimaces. "Horrible. Last night my family and the Hamptons went to the church together and listened to Mrs. Bette play the organ. It was the first time Clyde and I have sat next to each other in years, and his breath smelled like soured milk. His conversation was just as bad."

The thought of Clyde sitting by Ruth in a church pew boils my blood. I hold up a hand. "It makes me sick thinking of it."

"Oh, I wasn't trying—"

"I know," I interrupt and put my hand into my pocket to pull out her hanky. But before I do, the front door downstairs slams shut. Nurse Mabel's hearty voice fills the building. "If we can't raise the money selling livestock, how will we afford to build the addition?"

"The Lord will provide," Preacher Docket says in his singsong way. "As always."

Wild-eyed, Ruth whispers, "You have to hide.

Quickly. There's no way down the stairs but past the preacher."

I frantically look around the room. The bed is too close to the ground for me to squeeze under. The quilt stand would have trouble even just hiding my legs. Bounding into the hall, I see all of the other rooms are the same. The only bedroom that might be different is Preacher Docket's. Like Daniel being thrown into the lion's den, I open the door to his room and slip inside.

11. NO EAVESDROPPING

TWO WINDOWS, with curtains drawn wide, light up the room. One looks out to the east, the other to the south. A mahogany desk in the corner has an oil lamp on it, several stacks of paper, a handful of books, and a framed drawing of Preacher Docket that makes him look fifteen years younger. Apparently, he never was a handsome man. A rocking chair with a large, crocheted doily on the seat is at the end of the bed.

Even though the room is larger than the others, its hiding places are also scarce. At the opposite end is a door. Maybe a closet?

Footsteps on the stairs convince me not to take my time finding out. I open it and see clothes on hangers. Even though it's mostly full, I squeeze myself in and shut the door behind me.

A pair of footsteps enter the bedroom. Then another. Wooden chair legs scrape across the hardwood floor. Preacher Docket and Nurse

Mabel are in the room, only feet away from where I hide.

Dust settles in my nose, and I'm terrified I'll sneeze. I press my face into my shoulder.

"I hear talk you and Dirk Hampton are headed to Mexico next week to purchase land for the relocation." Nurse Mabel sounds annoyed.

The tickling in my nose doesn't stop. I force my face deeper into my shirt.

Papers shuffle. "There have been some negotiations," answers the preacher, his voice preoccupied.

"I'd like to come," she says, "to Mexico that is."

"No, I need you here to take care of things."

"But I always have to stay here. I need to replenish my medicine supplies," she argues. "There's licorice elixir for dysentery, whale blubber for psoriasis and—"

"Enough."

Luckily, my sneeze escapes at the very second moment Preacher Docket thumps the top of his desk.

"You can't come with us this time," he says. "Dirk can pick up the supplies you need. Make him a list."

Nurse Mabel clicks her tongue in disapproval. "Are you sure about that?" Her voice grows soft. I can hardly hear it. "Do you really want Dirk buying the kind of...*medicine*...I used on your father?"

The movement of paper abruptly stops. "I wasn't aware you were running out of that particular kind of *medicine*." Preacher Docket stands.

"On second thought, perhaps you should accompany us."

They speak in muted voices, like the wind when it whips in the trees at night. Something runs across the top of my shoe. The light from the crack at the bottom of the door shows it's a family of mice.

"Excellent," Nurse Mabel says triumphantly. "There's a lot of things I need from Mexico. Take for instance cough syrup. I can't prove it, but I'm sure Dillan Burnes stole a whole bottle of it."

"The boy's a thief," mumbles the preacher, "among other things. Why did he take it?"

"For his brother."

"Ah, yes, Joshua," he says. "And how is he?"

"Same, I suspect. I haven't seen him in a bit. You're the one who saw him last."

"Yes, I suppose I am. Tell me, what's really the matter with him?"

"Consumption." Nurse Mabel hisses the word as if by simply saying it she might catch the disease. "He'll go like the rest of them, but I see no reason to sound the alarm. The sickness is a natural thinning process to keep the strong, and rid ourselves of the weak."

Her words stab into my chest.

"And the spells the boy has? What are they?" asks Preacher Docket.

"I'm not positive, though my guess is a disease of the brain. I've read about it before."

At that moment, I want to reach out and strangle her. She talks about Josh like he's a piece of farm equipment that's breaking down.

"And you don't think his spells or the

consumption will affect the others?" Preacher Docket sounds only slightly interested.

"No."

"How long will he live?"

Nurse Mabel sighs. "The disease takes its time, slowly eating away at the body, sucking out life little by little. In the end, though, it'll get him. No doubt about it."

The preacher chuckles. "That sounds familiar."

"Well, now that you mention it, I guess it does sound like someone else we know." Nurse Mabel mockingly clicks her tongue. "Poor Docket Senior."

"It was my father's time to die," Preacher Docket says. "We just helped him do it quickly."

The truth hits me like a horse's hoof in the gut. Everything makes sense. The way Docket Senior suddenly fell ill. The way very few people were allowed to see him during in his last few weeks. The way Preacher Docket had become the next leader so quickly. It had all been the doing of Preacher Docket and Nurse Mabel. They had poisoned Docket Senior.

One of them snorts. It's a sickening noise.

"Good thing we got rid of him before he could denounce his son for adultery, lying, and blasphemy," says Nurse Mabel.

"And I'll get rid of anyone else who tries to stop me and my plans for the Departure." Preacher Docket adds, "It was for the greater good."

It's like listening to Cain justify the murder of

his brother Abel. I catch my breath as I think about the Bible story of the first killing. One act that started all of the evil on Earth. What if Docket Senior's death was only just the beginning?

The unmistakable sound of Preacher Docket's shoes moving across the floor sends chills up my body. "I need to make an example of a family in this town who has defied me. It will show the others not to resist. The Burnes would be perfect."

The doorknob to the closet wiggles. Light-headed, I press against the wall. I'm stronger and faster than either of them, yet the thought of them finding me cowering in a dark corner makes my muscles freeze.

Just then a scream sounds from outside the hotel and diner. "Help me!" It's Ruth. "Someone, please help!"

I have to stop myself from leaping out of the closet.

"What on Earth?" says Nurse Mabel, flinging open the window. She calls down below, "What's wrong, child?"

"I'm hurt," Ruth wails.

"Heaven sakes," Preacher Docket exclaims. "Her leg is covered in blood. Youth are so irresponsible these days."

"We'd better see what is going on."

I hear Nurse Mabel and Preacher Docket leave the room. Once they're gone, I hightail it from the closet and run toward the window. Carefully peeking over the ledge, I see Ruth on the ground. Her skirt is pulled up around her thigh, and on her leg is a gash above the knee as long as a slice of bread.

My head pokes out too far. Ruth sees me and waves furiously. Her lips form the word "Go." She then tilts her head backward and commences bawling. She's helping me get out of the room unseen.

Ruth's father, Nurse Mabel, and Preacher Docket arrive at her side.

"What did you do to yourself?" asks Preacher Docket, not an ounce of compassion in his voice.

"I fell and cut myself. It hurts!"

Moments later I bolt down the stairs, across the sitting room, and out the front door, smacking into the drooping chest of Nurse Mabel. She's come back inside, probably to fetch her medicine bag.

"What are you doing in here, boy?" she asks.

My mind tells my mouth to stay quiet, but it doesn't listen. "You killed him. You helped Preacher Docket kill his own father. You don't have a soul."

Her mouth drops open.

I push her aside and words flash in my mind.

Get.

Out.

Of.

Docketville.

Now.

12. NO RUNNING IN THE STREETS

AS MY FEET pound on the hardened, dirt road, Preacher Docket's words haunt me. *I need to make an example of a family. The Burnes would be perfect.*

That evil man is going to do something to my family, but I won't let him.

Not even over my dead body.

Morning air whips across my face. I run fast, faster than I ever have before. I'm getting Ma and Josh out of here. We're leaving Docketville for good.

I wish I had found the trail to Phoenix, but it doesn't matter. I will find the city on my own. I'll head northwest and trust my instinct—just like Pa taught me to do. I know these hills as well as anyone in town. Probably better.

"Dillan! Hey, hold up! What's your hurry?" Frank runs beside me and grabs my arm, forcing me to slow down. "You look like you've seen a ghost."

I stop and bend over, panting. Oxygen would do me good. "I…I'm leaving."

My friend's eyes widen. "Leaving what?"

"Docketville. For good." I gulp down air. "Josh has consumption. He's dying. And Preacher Docket and Nurse Mabel…they're killers. They poisoned Docket Senior. I heard them say they did."

"Poison?" Frank drops my arm. "Are you kidding me? You sound like you're going mad."

"I'm mad all right," I say, balling my fists, "but not the kind you're thinking of. Preacher Docket and Nurse Mabel are powermongers—the kind Docket Senior used to warn us about. And they know that I know what they did. I have to get my family out of this place before they decide to kill me too."

Frank shakes his head. "No, Dillan. You're not feeling well."

I lift my head up and stare point blank into the eyes of my best friend. "I know what I heard. I swear it…on the Bible."

Swallowing hard, Frank stands a little taller. He clasps my hand. "What can I do? How can I help?"

I take a deep breath, readying myself to run again. "If they come looking for us, hold 'em off as long as you can."

He pulls me closer and slaps my back like we're brothers. "I'll do it. And, Dillan?"

"Yeah?"

"Get out of here, fast!"

———

I fling the door to our house open. Ma is inside, stacking wood by the fireplace. Josh is cleaning out the kindling pail. They move so slowly. They don't know what I do.

"We have to get out of Docketville!" I yell, sprinting to the kitchen and grabbing my hunting bag from the corner.

Ma stands and hugs her waist like she's got a sick stomach and just might lose her breakfast. "What's happened?"

I wish I could spare her from the truth, but she won't follow me if I do. I have to tell her everything. "At the hotel and diner I overheard Preacher Docket and Nurse Mabel talking. They said they killed Docket Senior. They fed him some sort of medicine that was really poison. It's no lie, Ma. They're murderers."

Josh's face wrinkles in confusion, like he's trying to swallow a goose egg whole. Ma's, however, turns into a sheet of fear.

"Do they know you overheard them?" she asks.

I nod. "I...I told Nurse Mabel that I knew what she'd done."

Ma gasps.

"That's not all. Preacher Docket is planning to make an example of our family. We have to get out of Docketville." I shove my canteen into a bucket of fresh water on the counter. It seems to take forever for the bubbles to rise to the surface, telling me the bottle is filling up.

Within seconds Ma has thrown open the pantry door and is pulling out food. "You're right, Dillan. Bad things are happening. You boys have to leave."

"We all have to leave," I say.

"Josh," Ma calls out, "go to your bedroom and get some warm clothes. The mountains are cold at night."

As my brother leaves the room, she turns back to me and says quietly, "I'm not going. I'll never make it. You'll have your hands full with Josh. If I stay here, I know I can convince Preacher Docket to leave you two alone." Her eyes plead with me. "Go to Phoenix and get Josh to a doctor. Please, Dillan. Do it for me."

I can't believe she's saying this.

Leave Ma behind?

With a murderer?

Impossible.

"You're not listening to me!" I yell. "You're coming with us."

Ma holds my hands in hers. "I'm not," she whispers. "I can do more for both of you here than I ever could in the mountains. I'll meet you in Phoenix later. But for now, you two have to go. Please, save your brother."

I remember what Nurse Mabel said about Josh wasting away to nothing. Maybe there was hope for my brother in Phoenix. But how could I leave Ma? My heart feels like it's going to rip in two.

She grips my shoulders. "Dillan, you were born for this. You can do it." And then she hugs me, her body shaking in my arms.

"All right," I say. "I'll do it. I'll save Josh. But,

Ma, you have to promise me you'll find us in Phoenix soon."

She wipes her eyes with her apron. "I will."

But something tells me she's lying.

13. NO NAPPING

WITH EACH STEP, Josh and I leave everyone we know behind: Frank, Ruth, and Ma. And of course, Preacher Docket. The more distance between him and us the better.

We hike in full afternoon sun, taking only small sips from our canteen, knowing that the sun's heat will be relentless tomorrow as well. Josh isn't a fast hiker, but he's determined. Step by step. Labored breath after labored breath. We find ourselves on Longhorn Mountain once again, but this time we don't stop at the outcropping of boulders to look for treasure. Instead, we keep on moving, spurred by the thought of a possible posse behind us.

Despite our quick start, it isn't long until we hear the sound of horses' hooves, shattering the silence of the wilderness.

"They're coming after us," I say.

"What are we going to do?" asks Josh, his eyes wide and frightened.

We can't outrun horses. Honestly, Josh could hardly outrun a cricket. I walk backward, sweeping away our tracks with sagebrush.

"Keep your eyes open," I answer. Truth is, I've no idea what to do. The vegetation is sparse in these parts. If we could climb farther up the mountain we could hide in a clearing of pines. But judging how loud the noises from the horses are, there isn't time.

"Dillan!" Josh points at a badger exiting a hole dug into the side of a slope. "We can hide in there."

My brother shimmies into the tunnel like a snake returning to its den, but I'm a different story. My shoulders don't fit in straight, so I tilt them sideways like an unbalanced scale and inch my way forward. Visions of the men finding my legs and buttocks sticking out of the earth keep me moving.

Clawing my way into the badger's sett, I start to feel funny like I'm going to faint. There isn't enough space for my lungs to fill with air. My head spins, and my ears buzz something fierce.

"Josh," I call ahead, "you keep going. I have to go back. I don't fit."

"But they'll catch you," he protests. "You aren't going to be caught by a bunch of lawless men. There's more room the further you go in. Promise."

I do it for him. I blow out every last bit of air from my lungs and swivel my shoulders side to side, covering myself with dirt. Little by little I ease forward, wishing the image of a horse giving birth would get out of my head.

I'm sure I'm going to be stuck like this forever when I feel Josh's hands take a hold of mine and pull. I don't know where he gets his strength, but it's enough to pop my shoulders out and into a cavern six feet wide and three feet tall. After being in that awful tunnel, it feels like a rich man's mansion. Curled up, I fit in the space along with Josh at my side.

Sunlight from the outside reveals grass and dead leaves and animal droppings that cover the floor of the cavern. Near one side is a thick tree root with claw marks all over it. Several other underground tunnels shoot off the main den where we're hiding. Even though we're out of sight from Preacher Docket's posse, we're not out of danger yet. We might have ourselves an angry badger to deal with soon enough; something I don't look forward to seeing how I can't even move my arm in front of my face.

"They're never going to find us in here," Josh says, moving his pack and my bow and arrows so I have more room.

"That was good thinking, Josh," I say, and I mean it. We would have been caught for sure.

A few minutes later, the ground shakes, stirring up puffs of dirt outside the sett. A man's shout travels into the tunnel.

"I thought the footprints were headed down the other side," says Dirk Hampton. "We're on the wrong trail."

"Nah," someone else answers. "Those tracks weren't fresh. We're in the right place."

The two exchange a few heated words until another man chimes in. "We ain't getting very far arguing. Let's split up. Half of you should follow Dirk to the other side, and the rest of us will go with Peter. We'll meet up at Elk's Wash."

The men voice their agreement, and the horses start up again. I peek at Josh, worried he might be feeling scared. His eyelids are shut and he's sleeping like a baby. Not a bad idea. Using my satchel as a pillow, I curl up and join him for an afternoon nap.

The air tastes dry when I wake. I've no idea how long we slept, but judging from the cramping in my legs, it was too long. Josh snores peacefully at the moment, though there is a puddle of dark liquid by his mouth. Blood.

"Wake up, Josh," I say, jostling his shoulder with my foot. "You can't sleep all day. What would Ma say?"

"Ahh." Josh yawns. He wipes the red spittle from his lips and smiles. "And a good morning, or should I say afternoon, to you too," he says.

"Sleep well?" I ask, eying the result of what must have been some pretty serious coughing in his sleep.

"Like a baby," he answers. "I don't know about you, but I'm ready for some food."

Josh gets out the food and we slowly chew on jerky and take small sips of water as we listen out the opening of the badger sett. Nothing stirs. I dread leaving, mostly because the tunnel looms before me like the eye of a needle a camel must walk through before getting to heaven. No wonder I won't make it to paradise. I don't do well with small spaces.

Getting out of the sett is easier than it was

going in. Josh braces himself for the best possible leverage and pushes me from behind. I wiggle and squirm and am thrilled to reach the open air.

"Which way?" Josh asks.

"Northwest," I answer, pointing to a cliff on the side of the mountain in front of us.

"What?" he answers. "Don't you think we should skirt around that steep part and save ourselves some grief?"

"Nope," I insist. "Have you ever seen a man on horseback scale a rock wall like that before?"

Josh shakes his head no.

"That's why we're going to."

———

The cliff looks more menacing every step we take. Josh looks at me like I'm crazy, and maybe I am. When we arrive at the base, I study the cliff like I do a piece of wood before carving it. I check for natural grooves, jutting slabs of rock, or holes and blemishes. In carving, those things add character to the figure. In climbing, they'll keep me alive.

"Over there," I say, pointing to the left, "is the best way up."

Josh hasn't stopped coughing in over an hour, yet his face is all smiles. "Oh, come on," he says, "quit fooling me. Just say you made a mistake when you thought about climbing this canyon wall, and I won't rub it in...at least, not that much."

"No mistake," I grunt. "You take this." Before handing Josh the pack and the bow and arrow, I take another drink from the mostly empty canteen around my neck. Wiping my sweaty palms on the front of my dirty pants I tie the rope Josh brought with him around my waist and begin. Above me, a hawk cries out. I take it as a welcoming call. The sun beats on my arms as I find my first handhold. Pulling my body close to the rock, I pull upward. In the past, while out hunting treasure, I had scaled walls—fifteen, maybe eighteen feet tall. But this cliff is no less than fifty feet high with one lone ledge to stand on midway up.

Josh stands below me, petrified. "Even if you make it, I can't. Are you going to leave me for buzzard food?"

A pair of flies try to distract me. I ignore them like I do Josh. Push left, pull right, I tell myself. Steadily I move upward like a lizard, winding back and forth on the wall. A few feet below the ledge, my foot slips and I skid down the rock face, barely just catching a branch of a bush growing out of a crag before losing complete control. Hanging there reminds me of the laundry line Ma uses to dry our shirts and underwear on in the summer.

I pull myself up using the bush and find a new handhold. There's only a little bit more to go before I can rest on the ledge and pull Josh up halfway.

When I reach the small landing spot, Josh whoops and yells.

"Quiet!" I order.

Embarrassed, he puts his hand over his mouth, and I hide my own smirk. Pride is of the devil, which is probably why I feel so much of it right now.

I lower the rope to my brother, and he ties it under his shoulders, strapping all of our gear to his back. It's a thin rope, and I thank my lucky stars Josh weighs near nothing. I pull slowly, not wanting to hit him against any sharp rocks.

"Push off the side every so often," I softly call down.

"Will do," he answers. He's so excited that his lungs forget to cough for a minute.

First his hands, holding onto the rope for dear life, and then his head pops above the rock ledge I'm standing on.

"Get that silly grin off of your face," I say. "We're not out of the woods yet."

"But," he laughs, "that was fun."

The second half of the cliff has a more gradual slope, and I make it up to the top without too many problems. My hands are so tired from climbing I'm afraid I won't be able to keep hold of the rope to pull Josh up. Just to be safe, I tie it around the trunk of a sycamore and throw the other end down to my brother. A minute or two later he tugs it, letting me know he's ready. Twenty hefty pulls later I've just about got him to the top when there's a clatter below.

My heart skips a beat. "What happened?" I can't see over the edge.

"The bow and packs," he answers. "They all fell."

"How far down?" But from the sound of Josh's voice, I already know.

"All the way to the bottom."

I stop pulling on the rope. The thought of our gear so far below us makes me sick. Our rope isn't long enough for me to get back down. The cliff face is too sheer to climb backward. And we've not got the luxury of wandering around the mountain looking for a drop in. We've got a posse on our tail. There's nothing to do but push forward to Phoenix.

"Can you get me up?" Josh's voice is timid.

I'd forgotten he's hanging almost fifty feet in the air.

When Josh makes it to the top of the cliff, he's teary-eyed. "I'm really sorry. There was just so much to carry and I—"

"No use crying over spilled milk," I say. But it doesn't come out as nice as when Ma says it. Probably because she means it and I don't. All Josh had to do was hold on to a few things. He didn't have to do anything else. It wasn't that hard.

Now what?

All we have to get us to Phoenix is my canteen, a rope, my pocketknife, and a gold nugget sewn into my pants.

Josh hangs his head.

I shrug and start walking. My mouth is dry, and with every step I hear the quiet slosh of the few tablespoons of water at the bottom of my canteen.

———

There's been no sight of a stream, pond, or even a trickle of water. To stave off thirst, I suck on a handful of juniper berries, though they're nothing like real berries—just hard little balls that have a bitter taste. But having something in my mouth tricks my throat into thinking it's not parched.

Several hours later, on my command, Josh swallows the last bit of water. It gurgles down his throat, and I try to ignore the sound. My stomach rumbles but I hardly pay attention. Who wants food when there's nothing to wash it down with?

We don't see the posse the rest of the day. Without a word between us, we hunker down for the night, curling around a small fire. I fall asleep to the howling of coyotes in the distance and Josh's coughing in my ear. I dream of waterfalls, lakes, and the well behind the house, but, in the morning, I'm still thirsty.

14. NO DRINKING

IN THE EARLY MORNING HOURS, Josh shakes me awake. "I had a fit while I was sleeping, Dillan. I don't like that." He shivers.

"You're going to be okay," I answer, wishing he would go back to sleep. "We're going to get you to Phoenix, meet Ma there, and live happily ever after."

Josh looks me straight in the eye. "That's a lie. We're never going to see Ma again."

I frown.

Josh continues, "She's going to marry Preacher Docket and go live in Mexico."

This was news to me. Stunned, I ask, "Why would Ma marry Preacher Docket and go to Mexico?"

"You know how I once told you I had a secret that I didn't know if I should tell or not?" Josh looks down.

"Yes."

"Well, Preacher Docket likes Ma," he stammers.

"What do you mean he likes her?"

Josh squirms. "Likes her...like a man likes a woman."

I stare, hearing his words but not understanding them.

"A few days after Pa died, Ma and I were the only ones home. Preacher Docket didn't know I was there. He came into the house, and right there in our kitchen he told Ma he loved her and that the two of them should run away together to Mexico. He said it was part of...The...the D-Departure, I think."

"Preacher Docket said he loved Ma?" The very idea makes me sick to my stomach.

"Yes. He...he kissed her. It made her cry."

I gasp. "And you never told me?"

"No." Josh starts to cry.

"Josh!" I don't realize I yelled his name until I see the fear on my brother's face. "Why didn't you say anything?"

He shakes his head ferociously back and forth. "After Preacher Docket kissed Ma she slapped him, really hard. He yelled at her and said he'd have her whether she liked it or not. And then he...he hit her. More than once. It...it was bad. I was so scared I hid in my room. I'm...I'm a coward."

"Hit her!" My chest is about to explode with hatred.

"Before he left the house, Preacher Docket threatened Ma that if she told anyone about what happened, especially you, Dillan, he'd—" Josh makes a choking sound.

"He'd what?"

"—he'd kill her." The words hang in the air like the stench from a dead carcass.

My anger builds until I'm a scalding pot of potatoes ready to boil over. No wonder Preacher Docket hates my family so much. Ma had refused his advances point-blank. Even when he threatened her.

The man was going to burn in hell.

"Josh," I say, "Ma will not marry Preacher Docket. I'm going to get you to Phoenix to see a doctor. A real doctor. Not like Nurse Mabel. And then I'm going to get Ma, even if I have to walk to Mexico and bring her back myself."

———

By afternoon, I want to give up. "There might not be any water in these mountains."

"There's got to be," Josh rasps. "We've seen deer and rabbits. Even some wildflowers. If they're here, there's got to be water. We'll make it."

That's my brother. Lying on the ground, covered with dirt and dried spittle, telling me everything's going to be just fine.

"No doctor in Phoenix can help you if you're dead," I answer. "They're not miracle workers, you know."

I wait for a response. None comes. I look over and he's sleeping. Flies swarm around his sweaty face like they would a rotting animal. I shoo them away. I can't leave my brother here in the mountain heat. He may never wake up. We have to keep going.

Knotting the rope like I did when carrying Samson on my back, I make a net. I place Josh in the middle of it, hoist him onto my shoulders, and strap him to me. He wakes up and tells me to knock it off, that he can keep walking, and that he doesn't want to be carried like a baby in a papoose. I ignore him.

Chewing on the roots of rattlesnake weeds and monkey flower leaves, I trot through the brush. It's not exactly what you'd call food, but it distracts me a little from my hunger pains and the heat. Nothing, though, can take my mind off of water.

The lower portion of the mountain is forested in patches. Further up, the trees become dense with a promise of shade and maybe even a stream. For a long while, Josh doesn't stir. I worry he's dead, that his soul's in heaven with Pa's.

Like a hen that can't stop brooding for its chicks, I stop and try to calm my breathing so I can listen to his. He's a sleeping sack of bones on my back. The exact opposite from Samson's plump, rotund body.

I promise myself I'll carry Josh all the way to the hospital in Phoenix if I have to. He's all I have. Any anger I felt over the lost supplies is gone. I just want my brother. Alive.

Burrs the size of corn kernels cling to my pants and socks, scratching my flesh with every step. The sun sucks the last bit of water from my mouth, throat, and tongue. I can't even blink. My eyelids scratch my eyes like sandpaper. Cold water, warm water, clean water, dirty. It doesn't matter. I'd take any kind right now.

A coughing fit from Josh assures me he's still breathing. For now.

A bird soars overhead, flying into the setting sun. Even though I've slowed down, time hasn't. It's hardly a fair race. Within minutes the temperature falls, and I start to shiver. At least being thirsty in the cold is better than during the heat of day.

Using a flat stone and my bare hands I dig a shallow trench. I line it with rocks the size of plums and start a fire inside. One full day of walking, coughing, and starving, but no water. How much more can we go?

When the rocks are hot, I smother the fire, remove the coals, and cover the stones with soft leaves and brush. Gently, I set Josh into the warm pit. His sunburned skin, disheveled hair, and blood-splattered face remind me that I'm no pretty picture to look at either. If Ruth could see me now, she'd swear on the Holy Writ that I'm a demon for sure.

Halfway through the night, I decide it would be better to walk in the dark than worry while not sleeping in the cold. I put Josh on my shoulders again. He mutters something and then quiets down. Gratefully, the moon is out nearly in full. I trudge up the mountain.

The going is slow, but it's something. It's one more foot, one more inch, closer to water. To survival. To life.

I track my direction with the stars and

remember the first time Pa showed me how to find the Big Dipper. I was five, maybe six, and we were sitting out on the porch with me on his lap and Ma at his side. Now I wish I'd never grown older, never become a sinner, and never gone into Preacher Docket's bedroom and learned the truth. The thought of Preacher Docket's name makes me picture what it must have been like for Josh to have seen the preacher kissing Ma in our kitchen. It makes me gag even though I have no spit in my mouth. Will I ever see Ma again? The emptiness inside me is as big and dark as the night sky.

The first of Josh's fits begins near daybreak. At first he groans, and I don't think much of it. The next thing I know, he's jerking about, legs kicking me like an angry cow during milking.

"Josh!" I call out, but he can't talk. After a minute or so the violent movements turn into twitches. Slow and steady. Fear explodes inside me. I have nothing. I am nothing. I have no bottle of medicine, no soft bed, not even a cool sip of water to offer him. He's dying, and I just plod on like a pathetic animal carrying its load. Two more fits, one after another, and by the end of them Josh's body is as limp as a gutted fish.

More sun. More heat. More silence.

I start seeing people about lunchtime. Pa's there and I'm madder than a hornet, giving him a piece of my mind for leaving—as if he had any say in dying.

Next, I see Ruth. She's dressed how she was that day in the barn when we almost kissed. Instead of me, though, she's pushed up against

Clyde and they're cooing at each other like two lovebirds in a nest.

I shake my head, not sure what's real and what isn't. "Water," I say aloud to no one but the blue sky. I know I won't last another day without a drink. Panic rises inside me when I think of someone finding our dead, rotting bodies in the mountains. Ma deserves better.

Falling to the ground is the easy part. Getting Josh off my back is even more tricky. Getting both of us under the shade of a tree is the hardest. All I want to do is close my eyes and sleep.

I awaken to the sound of a doe trespassing on our hiding place. Where are we? What direction are we headed? The last thing I want to do is mistakenly walk back to Docketville.

Remembering a trick Frank once showed me, I poke a stick into the ground, marking the end of its shadow. Then, curling up next to Josh in the shade, I wait for the shadow to shift positions. The sun is reliable as always. After fifteen minutes or so, the shadow has moved several inches to the right. I draw a line between my two marks, which gives me an east-west line. Phoenix is northwest. That means we have to cross over the towering mountain in front of us.

No need to wait. There's nothing but thirst here.

I gather my bearings and get back on my feet. Josh has turned a strange shade of gray. Ma would have said it reminded her of a baby jackrabbit, but I think he looks like a stillborn calf. She's always trying to make things look better than they really are. That's the difference between me and her.

Hours pass. My daydreams about water are unrelenting. First, I see it bubbling up from the earth into a dry bed of rocks. It's small but grows into a stream the width of a wagon. I imagine walking through it, feeling its guilty pleasure on my feet, basking in the wetness on my skin. I dip my hands into it, lean over, and lick the drops off my fingers like a dog cleaning its newborn pup. Surprisingly, the water feels like fire on my tongue, scorching my throat.

I'm not sure how long I'm there, licking water off my hands, until I realize I'm not dreaming. It's real, as real as the pain in my head and the throbbing in my gut.

"Ahh," I shout, sounding like a madman. I fall into the wetness, opening my mouth wide and letting a flood inside.

Then I remember Josh. Forcing myself out of the stream, I lay his body under a tree. He doesn't move. Taking off my shirt, I rinse it out in the stream and then fill it up with the liquid. I drip some into his mouth, over his forehead, in his hair, everywhere. He stirs and pokes his tongue out like baby robin begging its mother for a worm.

I wipe the dried blood from his face and hands. He licks his lips. I wring the shirt and water falls into his mouth like a waterfall. He gags so I slow down. His eyes open for the first time today.

"Mo..."

It's not a word, at least not one that I understand, but it tells me he's back with me for the moment.

"More?" I ask. He nods.

I return to the stream, gulp down what seems like a milk bucket full, and then fill up my shirt again. We drink and drink; me swallowing mouthfuls at a time, and Josh sipping spoonfuls. In the end, Josh is the smarter of the two of us. Less than a quarter of an hour later I'm bent over on the moist ground covered with pine needles, reeling in pain. Cramps travel from my gut into my legs. All I can do is whine like a nursing pig.

Josh, who is able to sit on his own, leans back on the bumpy trunk of an evergreen and holds my hand. We stay like that until evening turns— me, thinking I'm going to die, and Josh, who actually may die, comforting me.

Like the calm after a storm, my stomach returns to normal. Using a low hanging limb from an enormous ponderosa for cover, Josh and I spoon together under his blanket and let the dark overtake us. This night I dream of food.

15. NO GLUTTONY

ON THE FIFTH day of creation, God made the creatures of the sea. While I'm grateful for that, I do wish he'd made them a little slower. It takes me almost an hour to catch a trout with my bare hands. I gut it and roast it on a stick over a small fire. I feed Josh first, but he can't keep down a single bite.

When we were sick as children, Ma made us the best chicken soup. While we may not have chicken, I figure a little fish broth couldn't hurt Josh.

Using my pocketknife, I carve a bark bowl by placing some hot coals on a piece of aspen I've whittled down to the thickness of lye soap. I scrape away the middle of the charred wood until it scoops down nice and low in the middle. Next, I put water, a piece of raw fish, some shriveled hackberries, and hot pebbles into the makeshift bowl. Within minutes I've made something like a fish stew. I strain the pebbles and berries out with my fingers, eat the chunks of cooked trout, and then tip the bowl into Josh's mouth. He reaches up and holds it close to his lips, drinking it like manna from heaven. And just maybe it is.

I get better at catching fish and collect a mess of them by lunchtime. We stay hidden by the water for several more hours, drinking, eating, and napping to our hearts' content. I feel guilty. This is the exact spot where Preacher Docket and his men will search for us, but every time I look at Josh, I don't want to move him. He looks thin enough to snap in two. I make more stew, and he drinks it greedily. A little color comes back to his face, breaking through the awful dull gray.

Late afternoon sneaks up on us, and it's time to go. No excuses. We eat our fill, rub white powder off the trunk of an aspen tree on our faces to block the sun's rays, fill the canteen, and start off again.

For the most part, I carry Josh in my arms since the ropes have rubbed some of his skin raw. Every once in a while he has the energy to get down and shuffle a bit. I tell him not to, but he does it anyway. Truth is, it makes me happy to see him moving. If he's moving, he's alive.

My belly sloshes as I follow the stream that winds closer and closer to the mountain peak. The aspens thicken near the top of the slope, and the pines perch like giants over the canyon below. I slow my pace as the slope turns steep.

"How far till Phoenix?" whispers Josh. His words are slurred, and his face is flushed with fever, but he's talking. Again, I take comfort in even the smallest things he does.

"Don't know," I answer. While it's true I don't know *exactly* how far it is, I do know we're nowhere near close. Pa and I did the math once and figured Phoenix was about one hundred twenty miles away from Docketville. Josh and I've gone fifteen, maybe twenty at the most. The numbers are too depressing to say out loud.

We walk on. As the moon settles, something on the banks of the stream catches my eye. It's high time for a rest, so we make our way over to it. There, lying on the ground, are the remains of a camp. There's a blanket, some cooking utensils, and…human body parts.

Torn flesh reveals protruding bones, like broken bloody stumps. Shredded clothing is scattered next to what must have been a man's boots. Josh scrunches his nose at the sickly, sweet smell.

Vomit fills my mouth. I spit it out. I need to get Josh away from the sight, but the call of a warm blanket and the chance of food force me to stay. Setting my brother down, I grab the blanket off the ground as well as a knife near the fire pit. They will help keep us alive later.

"What happened here?" Josh asks in a weak voice.

A low growl answers his question. No more than twenty feet away is a black bear, standing upright on its hind legs. She looks majestic in the moonlight—about my height, but twice my width.

I'm no match. She could eat me as a snack. Seeing how fresh the mangled body parts are, I pray she's already had dinner and just wants a cozy place to rest for the night.

Her dark silhouette frames two yellow eyes, and when she opens her mouth, a row of sharp teeth shine in the night. Another snarl tells me I'm the intruder here.

Whimpering, Josh gropes his way next to me.

"Quiet," I order him, "and don't let go of my leg."

Holding my hands in the air to make myself look bigger, I talk like I do to a spooked piglet.

"I'm awful sorry to barge in like this," I say and lower my eyes. "We're just leaving."

I take a step backward, snapping a twig when I put my foot down. The heavy-set bear takes a step toward me.

Each time I move so does it. Each step I take, every gesture I make, the bear mimics, all the while heading closer in our direction. It doesn't take long to catch on. It's playing with its food. I hold my stance, arms held high. The only part of me that moves is my chest, which jumps up and down like oil in a hot pan. A few minutes in that position and my already exhausted shoulders begin to shake. The bear is winning.

I lower one arm, hoping to relieve my muscles, when the bear rounds its back, ready to pounce.

"Dillan?" Josh chokes on my name.

His voice seems to wake something inside the furry beast. She howls a guttural yell and lunges. A foot or two from us, she stops, turns her head, and sniffs the air.

As I wait for my heart to start beating again, I hear what stopped her attack. A horse neighs in the distance. A man's voice rises above the trees.

"Jake?"

I know that voice. It's Dirk Hampton.

"I'm sure our camp was around these parts," he calls out. "Jake? Where are you?"

Jake Simmons is—was—the baker at the co-op. His sourdough bread is a legend. Without meaning to, my eyes fall on what is left of him. I want to upchuck the fish from that morning.

"Maybe Jake found the boys' trail and is following them," says another man.

The bear looks at me one last time, blinks, snorts, and—I swear it on the Holy Book— smirks. Then, without another sound, she's gone. Playtime is over.

Josh whimpers beneath me. I throw him over my shoulder and run blindly through the stream and into the trees on the other side. Branches whip my face. More than once I twist my ankle so badly I think I might have broken it. My breath comes in short hot bursts. Thoughts of the bear are gone. Instead, all I see in my mind is Preacher Docket finding Jake's leftovers and swearing his vengeance on me once again.

"Over here!" a man's frantic yell comes from behind.

Panting, I stop to listen.

"Help!" It's Clyde Hampton. Of course, he would join a search party bent on my demise. He's likely to pull the trigger himself.

"Jake's been killed." Clyde shouts. "He's torn apart."

A rush of voices follow but I don't wait to hear what they say. I charge into the dark, no idea what direction I'm headed except for away. I've been going for several minutes before it hits me that my load is lighter.

Where is my canteen and rope that I use as a net? I grimace when I realize I left them at the camp. Now I have nothing to help us get through the mountains. But even worse, if the posse finds my things, they'll know I'm close.

My leg hits a bush and I fall, doing the best I can to keep Josh from hitting the ground. I don't want to move. Sobs escape my throat. Loud ones that start in the deepest part of my soul and thunder outward. It's embarrassing, but I can't stop. It's over, I think. It's all over.

Josh squeezes my hand. With what must be his last bit of strength he says, "Dillan, please. Don't give up."

Struggling to my feet, I position him in my arms once again and move forward.

16. NO PROFANITY

I'VE GONE LESS than a tenth of a mile in the dark when the hollering behind me grows louder. One voice rises above the others, and it makes my hair stand on end.

"This rope is Dillan's!" Preacher Docket yells. "I've seen him make a net out of a rope like this before. John and Randall, you stay here and guard what's left of Jake's body. The rest of us need to spread out. The boy is close. I can feel it."

I push forward, telling my legs to move faster.

"What did he say?" asks Josh.

"Shh," I answer.

But it really doesn't matter. We can be as quiet as church mice, but it won't stop the men from finding us. No, what we need is a good old-fashioned miracle.

The trees thin, and before I know it we're in the middle of a clearing. We're sitting ducks. I steer to the left, heading back into the forest, when I see a tiny flickering beacon in the other direction across the expanse.

I'm a crazy fool for doing it, but I follow the light. I tell myself it could be a posse member holding a burning torch. Desperation pushes me forward.

Without any brush underfoot, I make good time. The closer I get, the more obvious it is that what I'm seeing is no torch. Soon I stand in front of the strangest looking cabin I've ever seen—something right out of a gentile's book of fairy-tales. The outside walls are just a hair taller than me, with a cedar shake roof on top. A chimney with smoke drifting out rises from one side of the cabin. The light I'd followed is a burning candle set against a tiny window no more than six inches wide.

Have I gone crazy? I reach out to touch it, just to make sure it's real, when the door swings open. I look down and see Arthur—one of the midget brothers.

My jaw drops.

Arthur grabs my arm and pulls me inside. I bend nearly in half to make it through the threshold. Once in the cabin, Arthur locks the door behind us and puts his tiny pointer finger to his lips.

The sign for quiet.

He doesn't have to show me twice.

Arthur and his brother, George, carry Josh to a miniature bed in the corner of the room. Instead of putting him under the blankets, they slide him under the box springs. To hide him even better, they push heavy wooden boxes in front of him.

George looks at me and points to the side of a large woodpile in one corner of the room. I shake my head, confused. Arthur pushes me toward it and motions for me to get down. I do, crouching as close as I can to the wall. George begins stacking the firewood on top of me.

The two brothers get a chair to pile the logs higher and higher—in front, to the side, and over my head. Outside, men's voices grow louder. Just as George and Arthur put the last log on the stack, there's a knock at their door.

"George? Arthur? It's Preacher Docket."

"Holy Mackinaw," exclaims George. He fumbles with the lock. A moment later the door swings open, hitting the wall.

"Have you got bats in your belfry, preacher?" asks Arthur. "You shouldn't be roaming the mountains on foot this time of night. They say Behemoth lives up here."

"Don't feed me that malarkey," answers the preacher. "Behemoth is a fictional monster from the Bible created in the imagination of overzealous preachers bound on frightening wayward children into obedience."

"Is that so?" George whistles a few times. "Here I thought every word in the Good Book was true."

"Gentlemen," Preacher Docket insists, "have you seen two boys near your place?"

"How old were these boys?" Arthur asks.

The door to the cabin slams shut. "Listen, George, Arthur, Docketville has always appreciated your support and more than generous business. As you know, we're a distinct people. A pure breed. But upon occasion, Satan does infiltrate our midst. There is evidence that my dear father, the man who created our town of love, serenity, and equality, was poisoned by a seriously deranged boy in our congregation. He's now trying to kill his younger brother the same way with medicine he stole from our town nurse."

Anger boils in me like a pot of water ready to douse a chicken before plucking. I swear under my breath. Preacher Docket knows how to twist the truth like none other. He is now framing me for the murder of his father!

"I hold no anger toward the boy," continues Preacher Docket. "I just want to help his soul. We're certain he's in this area. Have you seen him or his brother?"

"Anyone wandering these mountains this time of year has been turned to bear food by now," answers Arthur.

"The elder of the two is fourteen." Then Preacher Docket adds, "Though he's as big as most men and more cunning."

"Bears eat the big and small alike." George spits. A mouthful of chew lands on the floor.

"Are you telling me you haven't seen either of them?" Preacher Docket's condescending voice booms inside the cabin.

"We haven't," answers Arthur. "We're just poor ranchers trying to make a living."

"That's not what I've heard," says Preacher Docket. "I've heard you two have enough money to buy all of Arizona."

"And if that's true," says George, "what's it to you?"

Preacher Docket snickers. "It's just that I have a group of very angry men outside that are raring to find these boys. I sure hope none of them get some sort of fool idea and decide to shoot one of you two instead."

Just then, the sound of someone pulling back the rear set trigger on a rifle echoes in the small cabin. I can't see a thing, so I don't know who does it—the preacher or the midgets? If it's the preacher, and if he shoots George and Arthur, Josh and I are dead meat. The posse will tear this place apart and find us.

"I'm not frightened by you," says Preacher Docket, his voice low and deep.

"Sir," says Arthur, "you're wearing a mighty fine hat. It's going to be a shame to see a bullet go right through it."

The gun explodes, and I jerk, moving some of the logs on top of the pile.

On the other side of the cabin, something lands on the floor. The door bangs open.

"What's going on," shouts Dirk.

"How dare you ruin my hat," bellows Preacher Docket.

Next thing I know someone has opened a window. "Behemoth," shouts George. "Come here, girl."

I assume the midget brothers have trained themselves a ferocious dog of some sort—that is until I hear the screams of Clyde Hampton outside. "Have mercy on us. It's a bear."

A growl ricochets. A number of the men use foul words—definitely not Docketville approved.

"Mr. Docket," says Arthur, as calm as an evening wind in August, "if you leave now, we'll tell Behemoth to let you go. If you continue to make threats like a complete idiot, she will have a feast tonight."

"This is of the devil," Preacher Docket cries. "How have you possessed that bear?"

"Raised her as our own since she was a cub," answers George. "She's as loyal to us as Ruth was to Naomi."

Preacher Docket yells, "We're leaving. Come on, men."

Running footsteps fill the night air as George whistles and calls Behemoth's name once more.

My mind races. Is the bear inside the cabin? Will she want to eat me? After all, I'm not her friend.

"Everything's going to be all right." George speaks to the bear through the window. "You stay close, now, you hear, girl?"

And as sure as I'm hiding under a pile of wood, that bear bellows a noise that sounds just like "yes".

17. NO HORSE RIDING ON THE SABBATH

I CROUCH IN SILENCE, waiting for Arthur or George to make the first move. I worry they might have saved Josh and me to use as treats for Behemoth.

"Are you going to stay in that woodpile forever?" George asks.

"I sure hope not," I answer, my voice muffled. "I can barely feel my feet as it is."

One of the brothers lifts several logs off the top of the woodpile. I look around for a bear but there isn't one.

"Wh-where's the bear?" I ask.

"Outside." George slides boxes away from the bed to get Josh out.

"It killed the baker," I say. "Parts of him are still by the river."

"She couldn't have." Arthur grins. "Behemoth is as gentle as they come. It must have been one of her bear cousins. But Preacher Docket doesn't need to know that."

As George moves the boxes away from the bed. Josh pokes his head out. It sets him into a round of coughing. If he'd done that while Preacher Docket was here, we'd have been goners.

"You don't look so good, son," says Arthur. He pats Josh on the back, which does little except make a hollow sound echo inside my brother's body.

"I don't...feel so good either." Josh gags and coughs some more.

"Whoa there," Arthur steps back. "Sounds like we've got ourselves a lunger."

Before Arthur can say another word, I push the rest of the wood away from me and crawl over to where Josh lies on the floor. I prop him up and pull his back to my chest. Then, I wrap one arm around his front and place my other hand on his forehead. He lets me hold him like that while the hacking takes over every muscle in his body.

Deadly sounds rattle in my brother's chest. George shakes his head and clicks his tongue. Without a word, he tells me he knows my brother is dying. It puts a hornet in my britches. How dare he pass judgment like that? I haven't come this far to let him or anyone else tell me mine is a fool's errand.

"Sirs, I appreciate you for helping me and my brother out. But we need to be going." I stand up, as much as I can. The cabin ceiling is about two inches shorter than me.

"Not so fast, blue boy," says George, even though the coloring wore off weeks ago. "You're forgetting something important."

"What's that, sir?" I ask.

"Preacher Docket says you're a killer."

I laugh, which is probably what a person shouldn't do after being accused of a crime like that, but the whole thing is so...ridiculous. "Only if you consider slaughtering a pig or two as murder," I answer.

Arthur eyes me up and down. "You should know I can always spot a liar."

"Which must be why you didn't turn me into the preacher. That man is a walking lie. He's the one who poisoned his father. Not me."

Josh groans.

Arthur nods. "Set your brother on the bed and let's talk over a cup of coffee. I think your town is in some deep trouble right now."

The mention of coffee must prick Josh's interest because he opens his eyes. I hold him even tighter and sink to my knees. I never knew I could feel so tired.

As the brothers brew of a pot of strong coffee, they ask me what our plan is.

"I'm taking my brother to Phoenix. He needs a doctor." I hold my tongue, waiting for the midgets to laugh. To think that two bedraggled souls like us could walk all the way to Phoenix is certain to hit their funny bone.

But George doesn't laugh. Instead, he shakes his head. "Your brother doesn't need a doctor. He needs Edna."

"Who is Edna?" It was the same question I had wanted to ask back in Docketville when Frank and I had tried to help them with their horses.

"Edna," explains Arthur, "is our Ma, and she can cure anything."

The thought of George and Arthur having a Ma seems all wrong. I've always thought of them as just "being". Like they grew out of the dirt. What kind of woman would give birth to two midgets? A cursed one, most likely.

"You saved my brother from being killed by a horse," says Arthur. "I'd like to return the favor. We'll saddle up the horses and head east in the morning. She lives a bit out of the way."

"But," Josh begins, almost delirious, "tomorrow is Sunday and we're not supposed to ride horses—"

I stop my brother short. "We can ride horses just fine on a Sunday," I say. "The Rules of Docketville don't apply to us anymore."

I don't know what this Edna can do for my brother, but anywhere away from Preacher Docket sounds just fine to me.

———————

George and Arthur sleep on the floor while Josh and I enjoy their padded mattress. Even though my legs hang off the end by nearly two feet, it still feels like I'm surrounded by a billowing summer cloud. The cabin is warm from a black pot-bellied stove in the corner. Every few hours one of the midgets adds a log and the fire crackles, sending embers flying about. It reminds me of the fireflies Josh and I used to chase on hot August nights.

Sleep comes in waves. I dive deep into the

darkness only to be pulled awake from fear of drowning in its quietness. My body has forgotten how to rest. But it's all right. A fitful night in a bed is still better than sleeping in the open air on top of warmed rocks in a shallow-dug pit. In the early morning hours, my eyes pop open, and I jump out of the blankets quicker than if my bed sheets were ablaze.

"Calm down, blue boy," says Arthur, sitting in a miniature rocking chair. "Behemoth kept watch all night. Preacher Docket and his boys have gone for now."

I look around for George. He's not in the cabin.

"My brother's getting the horses ready," explains Arthur. "We'll leave after breakfast. It's two full days of riding."

———

Behind me, on the horse, Josh clutches my waist. The stallion we both ride trots at a hefty pace over a makeshift trail trappers and ranchers use to travel the mountains of Eastern Arizona.

"George," I shout above the noise of the horse's hooves, "why do you live in that tiny cabin when I'm pretty sure you two have enough gold to buy yourselves a mansion?"

"Who wants a big house when you're our size?" George answers. He and his brother share the other horse.

"I see what you mean." But I really don't. If I were rich, I'd want the biggest and the best. Fame. Fortune. All the fine things in life. Of course, I've never had a dime to my name, except for the gold nugget George gave me. So, what do I know of money? Only that I don't have it.

"We get tired of all the stares and jabs," adds George. "So, we like to keep to ourselves. Docketville isn't bad, though. You folks don't seem to care about our size as long as we spend money in your town."

Arthur speeds up. I follow his lead. The steady *clop* of the horses' hooves puts me in a trance of sorts. My mind takes me to things I want to forget. Ruth on the ground, her leg bleeding. Ma, shaking like a newborn robin and telling me to leave her. How did life become so complicated?

Josh is practically unconscious by the time we stop for the night. I volunteer to collect firewood to stretch my legs. When I return to camp, Josh is asleep on top of his bedroll. His dwindling body makes me want to count the minutes until we arrive at Edna's—though a big part of me wonders if the mother of two midget men can really help my brother. What will she look like? Will she be even shorter than the midgets?

When I get into my bedroll to sleep, I feel stir crazy and scared at the same time. Where do I belong? What do I do after Josh gets better? And will he get better? These are questions I've asked myself a lot lately. It hits me that maybe I don't belong *anywhere*. Maybe I just belong *to* someone.

Like Josh.

Ever since I walked into Ma's room and saw his brand-new body, all pink and wiggly, resting in the bassinet, I knew we'd always be together. It doesn't matter where I am if I'm with my brother. And that means one thing—my brother has to live.

Morning comes and we're back on the horses. Josh is doing worse. His breath is more shallow than usual, and his lips are blue. There is wet blood constantly in the corner of his mouth. It's like the world is full of air, but his body doesn't know how to breathe it in.

At lunchtime, Josh has five fits right in a row. All I can do is hold onto him and prod the horse forward. It knows something is sick on top of its back. It knows death is near.

There's no conversation. Only riding. Time is precious.

Over and over, I repeat to myself the promise I made to our ma. *I will do it. I will save Josh.*

And then, I ask myself, *can I save Ma?*

18. NO ADDRESSING ADULTS BY THEIR FIRST NAME

AS THE SUN sets and my body cools, George and Arthur call out, "It's around the bend. Careful, your horse might take off. These two like to gallop the final stretch."

Sure enough, a moment later our horse increases its speed. I fear I can't hold onto Josh any longer when the animal suddenly stops, nearly making me and Josh fly off the front.

Nestled in the mountainside is a cottage made of stone. It has solid rock pillars and a covered porch. The front door is plenty big for me to walk through without bending, and evergreens as tall as the church back home hug the gray walls. It reminds of a place near Docketville called Smuggler's Hideout.

The midgets stop their horse and leap from its back. "Edna!"

The front door opens and a woman almost as tall as my Ma walks out. She has gray hair, swept back in a bun, with a puzzle of wrinkles on her forehead and face. In her broad, thick hands she carries an empty bucket.

This couldn't be their mother. She looks so normal.

"Boys," she says, "you got here just in time to fetch me some—" she stops and stares at me, "—water."

"Edna," says George, "meet Dillan and Josh. The big one saved my life and we're repaying the favor. His brother is at death's door. Can you help him?"

The woman takes one look at Josh and ushers us inside. "Of course. Any friend of my boys is a friend of mine."

Within minutes, Edna has taken off Josh's shirt and is rubbing a thick yellow paste all over his chest. A handful of herbs steep in a cup of tea, and Arthur and George add something to the hearth that makes the room smell like a field after harvest.

"Thank you for helping my brother, uh...ma'am."

"Call me Edna," she says, brusquely.

"Yes, ma'am—I mean, Edna."

Putting her ear to his chest, she asks, "How long has he been like this?"

"Sick?"

"No," she responds, "practically dead."

"He's been really bad off ever since we left Docketville. That was about a week ago. But he's been sick for months."

"The toxins may be too strong," she mumbles as she wraps cheesecloth around Josh's torso. "If only he'd gotten here before the decay began."

Next, she rubs oils on his palms and the bottom of his feet. The smells in the stone house are overwhelming, and I begin to sneeze. Edna shoos me and the midgets outside. "Boys, fetch me water from the falls," she directs. "Not the well."

"All right, Edna," Arthur says. "Come on, blue boy. You're with me."

As we leave the cottage, Josh makes an unearthly wail. It's more noise than he's made in while. It gives me hope.

Arthur and I walk through the brush, dodging in and out of trees. The further from the stone house we go, the more I wonder where he's taking me. At last, we walk on a path made of flat stone that leads to a sheer mountain wall. A trickle of water runs down it. Where it comes from, I can't tell.

"*This* is the falls?" I ask.

"It used to be bigger. It's been drying up over the years." Arthur holds out his canteen and catches some liquid.

"Where's the source? Is something blocking it?"

"We've never been able to find the source. It comes from deep inside the mountain, I suppose. But this water is what kept Arthur and me alive as babes."

"You grew up here?" I ask, shocked. "Why?"

Arthur laughs. "If you haven't noticed, we don't look like other people."

I blush. "I know that. But I mean—"

"Right after we were born, Edna's husband—our pa I guess you could call him—threw her out of his home. He said she must have shared a bed with the devil himself to give birth to George and me."

What kind of a Pa would do that?

"Edna didn't have anywhere to go. She begged for money. Then one day a wagon party headed out west came through town. She joined them, but they were attacked by natives, and she was taken prisoner. When her attackers saw her two babes, even they didn't want her. They sent her on her way with a wagon full of supplies. She wandered in a haze until she ended up here at these falls. She's never left."

"But the house and the animals, where did it all come from?"

Arthur grins. "Have you ever heard of cattle rustling?"

"Yes."

"Let's just say George and I learned pretty quickly the tricks of the trade. Of course, we don't do that sort of thing anymore. Now we're legitimate."

So that was it. George and Arthur had been cattle thieves.

"Here, have a taste." Arthur pushes the canteen my way.

I take a swig and start to cough. The water tastes like a mix between a cow pie and cantaloupe. I've never tasted fresh mountain water like this before. "What's wrong with it?"

"Nothing is wrong with it. It's what is right with it. It comes from Mother Earth. Straight from her bowels." Arthur puts the cap on the canteen and begins walking back to the stone cottage. "If anything can bring life back to your brother, this can."

————

I can't stand the waiting and wondering of not knowing if Josh is going to live or not.

For the next five nights I sleep outside the stone house, keeping watch for Preacher Docket. Arthur and George tell me I shouldn't bother, but I can't stand being inside the cottage, listening to Josh's raspy breathing. During the days, I hunt with a bow the midgets let me borrow.

I sit on the porch and watch the rising sun. The night before I had hardly slept. Every time I got close to dozing off my mind reminded me of all my troubles—a dead pa, a sick brother, and a lost ma. Again, I promise myself I will find my mother just as soon as I can. My hands clamp around my biceps and my fingernails dig into my own skin. Preacher Docket will wish he never touched her.

The door behind me opens and Edna joins me outside with two bowls of mush. It's lumpy and sweet, with orange-colored nuts I've never tasted before. She sits next to me and eats her own breakfast silently.

I look closely at her and try to guess how old she is. From the straightness of her back, I'd say she's fifty. But looking at the deepness of her wrinkles, she seems more like a hundred. Then again, I have no idea how old the midgets are either. She calls them her "boys", but from what I heard in Docketville, the two of them have been running cattle for decades.

"Josh is a fighter," she says at last. "But you already know that, don't you?"

I nod.

"I know this isn't easy for you. I wish I could tell you he's going to make it, but I honestly don't know yet."

I wish she'd stop talking.

"My boys tell me you left your mother back home. Are you worried about her?"

I nod again. Thinking of Preacher Docket taking Ma to Mexico with him makes the mush turn sour in my stomach.

Edna eats another bite of mush. "My boys told me a little bit about this Preacher Docket. What do you think about him?"

She waits quietly for me to answer. I don't want to. I really don't. And then words start to spill from my mouth. "Preacher Docket is the devil himself. He makes rules to trap people. To make them follow him. To use people. To hurt them. Well, you know what I think? I think Docketville and its all rules can go to Hades."

Her mouth twitches. "I'm certainly no rule follower myself. I like doing things my own way, as you can tell." She waves her hand around her. "But not all rules are bad."

"I don't believe that." I set my bowl on the ground. "I've broken nearly every one of Preacher Docket's rules."

She shakes her head. "From what I've seen, I know you haven't broken the most important rule of them all."

I snort. "Oh, yeah? Which one is that?"

Edna pats my shoulder. "Be your brother's keeper. Josh is alive because of you."

A brother's keeper? I never thought of that being a rule. Rules are things you weren't supposed to do.

"Listen," Edna says, "I can't have you sleeping outside my house every night. You're mountain lion bait. You've done all you can for your brother."

I know she's right. It makes me out-of-my-mind crazy waiting around for him to get better. I don't know what to do with myself. My hands shake and my heart races even when I'm resting.

Edna stands up and brushes the dirt off of her skirt. "Dillan," she says, "your work is done here. It's time for you to help your ma."

19. NO BOYS IN GIRLS' BEDROOMS

LEAVING Josh is the hardest thing I've ever done. Even worse than leaving Ma. I fear I'll never see him alive again.

But I must leave.

The plan is for me to go back to Docketville and try and find where my mother is. The midgets say it should take me about a week and a half on foot. If Josh gets better, they'll need both horses to bring him to Smuggler's Hideout where Ma and I will meet Edna, Arthur, and George in three weeks. Edna says by then Josh will be better...or gone.

With plenty of food and water, I make great time traveling on my own. When I reach my home on the outskirts of Docketville, no one is there. I'm not surprised.

At home, the dishes are still in the sink from the night Josh and I left. The pantry is bare. I lift the rug that covers the cellar door and climb down. On the sparsely-filled shelves I find a few quart bottles of peaches and beans. I gulp the contents down, and the growling in my stomach relaxes.

I go back upstairs and into Ma's room. In the closet, I remove the loose floorboards and take Pa's best rifle out of the cramped space. It's three times the weight of the musket I own. Taking the gun and extra bullets with me, I head into my room and fetch my fishing knife. I slide it into a sheath tied around my waist.

Now it's time to figure out where Ma is. Frank might know.

I wait to go into town until near dusk. At the end of the main street there's a group of men standing about with rifles at their sides. They lean against posts and talk in loud boisterous voices. They are all strangers.

I walk up to the group, my hat pulled down.

"Whoa," one of them calls out in a strange accent. "What's your business this evening? It's getting close to curfew."

"Preacher Docket asked me to take a look at the pigs. Some of them have been acting sick," I lie.

"All right," the man answers. "But be quick. No one is out after dark."

"I won't be long." I head down the empty street in the direction of the pig pens. Who are these people and what are they doing in Docketville?

Once I'm out of sight of the guards, I make my way to Frank's house. A few candles flicker inside. A pair of his overalls hangs on the clothes-line outside. I put a note in the front pocket letting him know I'm back in Docketville and where he can find me. Frank will see the note soon since he only has two pairs of overalls, and he swaps them out every other day. Digging ditches is dirty work.

My next task won't be so easy. I sneak to my old stomping ground where a new litter of piglets squeal. I find a ladder and take it with me. Care-fully, I pass in between the buildings until I reach the end of the street and turn east, where Ruth lives.

I'm surprised to see the Ivins' porch lit with a kerosene lamp. Ruth sits on a bench next to no one other than Clyde Hampton. My hands go numb.

Setting the ladder down, I creep toward the couple and strain to hear their conversation. Clyde, of course, is mumbling. The imbecile never could talk halfway right. He's holding her hand—clearly breaking one of Preacher Docket's Rules. Ruth's head is lowered.

I'm so mad I itch all over.

Ruth pulls her hand away, scoots back, and stands up. "Time for me to get inside," she says. "Breakfast at the diner comes early."

Clyde moves closer to Ruth.

"I'm serious about going to Mexico. We have to go. Preacher Docket says there's no future in this forsaken place. He says Mexico has white sand and blue oceans, and it's the most beautiful place he's ever laid his eyes—"

Ruth interrupts. "I don't want to live there."

Clyde stands there like a dumb mule.

"Ruth?" Her father calls from inside the house. "It's past curfew."

"Coming," she answers.

Clyde takes a step forward and his lips head straight for her mouth. She turns her face at the last second, and he only brushes her cheek.

"The Rules," she hisses and retreats into the house.

My hands throb with heat, ready to land a punch square into Clyde's ugly face.

He gathers his coat and hat and saunters away. The urge to follow him and give him what he deserves tempts me. Instead, I take a seat underneath Ruth's second-story bedroom window. Beside me is the ladder from the pig pen.

When all of the lamps and candles in the house are out, I carefully place the ladder against the outside wall. I climb up it, grimacing each time a rung creaks. I reach the window, but inside her room is pitch black. I get as close as I can to the glass pane and whistle a tune we used to use as kids playing hide and seek.

I wait for what seems like enough time to have grown and harvested an entire field of corn. At last, there's movement. It's so dark I can't tell who it is. If it's Ruth's older sister, it'll be my day of reckoning.

The window opens slowly. I hold my breath until I see Ruth's face peer out. Dark circles surround her eyes, and she's a little thinner than I remember. Her hair is a little longer too, but still not anywhere near as long as a respectable girl's should be, according to Preacher Docket. The golden streaks in it reflect the moonlight.

"Dillan?"

Strange. I almost thought she might have forgotten my name. She says it again, soft and slow. This time it's less of a question.

I'd practiced my opening speech to her a million times on my way back to Docketville, but now that I'm here none of it sounds right.

"Y-You look good, Ruth," I say, stumbling over the words. She doesn't look good. She looks amazing. With thoughts like that, I'm sure I need repenting.

"You too."

In one gutsy move, I hoist myself onto the window ledge and into her bedroom. "I need to talk to you."

Her mouth turns into a smile—her smile. The one I daydream about. She reaches out and touches me as if to check whether I'm flesh or spirit. My skin lights on fire.

Ruth is wearing a white nightgown with big, puffy sleeves. Her older sister, Alice, is fast asleep in the double bed the two girls share.

"You've probably been wondering what happened to me," I say.

Ruth nods, never taking her eyes off of mine.

"I had to leave because Preacher Docket meant to harm my family."

Ruth drops her hand. "Preacher Docket said—"

"Whatever he said, it was a lie." I look straight

into her eyes. "I left is because I overheard a conversation he had with Nurse Mabel. They talked about how they killed Docket Senior with some kind of poison."

Ruth's mouth drops open and her eyes grow even wider. "Are you sure?" She leans in closer. I smell the familiar dish soap scent from the diner.

"Yes, I'm sure. When Preacher Docket realized I knew the truth, he sent out a posse to get rid of me...and Josh." Thoughts swarm my mind. There is so much I want to tell her, like how much it bugged me to see her with Clyde on the porch. But I need to find out about Ma.

Ruth shivers. "Preacher Docket told everyone you murdered his father, but I never believed it. And ever since you left, things have gone from bad to downright horrible in Docketville. Preacher Docket is a madman."

"*Horrible?*"

"Half of the town has migrated to Mexico on Preacher Docket's order. He wants to start a new Docketville down south. People who don't want to go—there's about ninety of us—are being punished. Distribution baskets have gotten smaller. People are going hungry. Preacher Docket has brought in guards—people he's hired from Mexico—to enforce town boundaries. No one is allowed to leave. It's like we're prisoners."

"I met a few of the guards earlier tonight," I say. "Not the friendliest bunch."

"Strange men meet the preacher at the diner," Ruth whispers near my ear. Her breath tickles my neck. "I hear some of what they say, and their conversations are anything but holy. And Nurse

Mabel is there. They all talk of power and control. It's shameful to see a woman so in love with money."

"But—"

She hushes me. "There's more. Preacher Docket turned the co-op building into a jail for dissenters."

"Dissenters?" I ask. "Like who?"

"Like your ma."

"My ma's in jail?" The words pummel me like a hailstorm.

"In front of everyone he accused her of being a vile sinner. It was the day after you left."

"But that was almost a month ago."

"I know." Her voice quivers.

I feel awful but relieved at the same time. At least I know she's not in Mexico.

"And Josh?" Ruth questions. "Is he alright?"

"Not sure," I answer. "He's with a healer named Edna. It's a long story."

Alice turns over in her sleep. She now faces us.

I don't have much more time. "Ruth," I ask, "did you give this to me?" From my pocket I pull out the white handkerchief that had once been folded into a dove.

She blushes. "I sure didn't leave it for Clyde Hampton."

A line of song's lyrics come to mind: *Love with a gentle persuasion.*

For the first time in my life, I'm absolutely sure she likes me, which makes me as nervous as a long-tailed cat in a room of rocking chairs. I feel like I'm back in the barn, not knowing where to put my hands or lips. But this time I don't hesitate. I lean in to kiss her, but she backs away an inch or two.

"We'd best not," she whispers.

Surprised, I stammer, "Oh, I'm sorry, I thought..."

Ruth frowns. "It wouldn't be fair to you. I won't be here too much longer. Pa doesn't want to go to Mexico, but he'll give in. Almost all the families have. We just don't have the means to take care of ourselves without Preacher Docket's help. I might never see you again."

My future dreams crumble like stale bread. "But I'll make sure you don't go to Mexico. I have a plan to—"

In her bed, Alice moans as if she's listening in her sleep.

Ruth's shoulders heave up and down. "There's nothing you can do. Preacher Docket has hired a small army from Mexico to force us all to leave."

I know what I have to do. "Then I'll make my own army." My words come out confident and loud. Too loud.

"Who's there?" Alice calls out in a half-daze, pulling back the bed covers.

I have only seconds. "Ruth, I..."

I want to kiss her. I really do, but I'm frozen to the spot.

She reaches up and holds my cheek in her hand.

Her tenderness is gentle and calming. So different from my actual life, and for a split second everything is better. But the moment is fast and hurried.

A scream interrupts my peace.

"It's him!" Ruth's sister Alice sits up in bed with the covers pulled to her chin. "It's Dillan Burnes!"

20. NO MONEY HOARDING

I FLY DOWN THE LADDER, three rungs at a time. Worried that Ruth will get into trouble if I leave any evidence of my visit, I tuck the ladder under my arm and run down the street. Alice's screams have stopped. They are replaced with her father's shouts.

"We have an intruder!"

I don't know what to do. Instinct urges me to go and break Ma out of jail this very instant. But what if I'm caught and locked up too? I'll be useless.

With the twelve-foot ladder at my side, it's impossible not to be noticed. The only thing I have going for me is a head start, but that's not enough. Three men rush out of the old post office.

One holds a lantern and yells. "There he is! Over there! And he's got...a ladder?"

Within seconds their footsteps sound in hot pursuit.

I dash into the space between the blacksmith's

and the tanner's. As I run, the ladder swings back and forth, hitting the sides of both buildings. It jars me each time and my pace slows.

Behind the tanner's shop hang several hides, some still wet. I dodge them, but the ladder catches one and pulls the clothesline down to the ground. I don't stop. Behind me snakes a rope with several animal skins attached.

Shouts from behind make me run all the faster. If I continue north about a mile, I'll reach the Christensen's farm. Maybe I can find a spot to hide there.

"You go to his left. I'll take the right." Two of the guards are upon me. I have no choice but to confront them. I swing about face and they nearly trip trying to stop in time.

"Come nicely," says one man in short breaths, "and I'll spare you a few bruises."

"If not, we'll make it hurt extra," says his partner who holds the lantern. "I promise."

The men advance, and I grip the ladder with both hands. When I swing it full force into their chests, they bellow in pained surprise.

The lantern falls to the ground along with both men. They wrap their arms around themselves and groan. I don't wait for others to come. I turn and run.

I sleep a few hours in the Christensen's haystack. Before dawn, I head to the hills. The sun is barely in the sky when I shimmy into the badger's sett Josh and I hid in before. Three times that morning a search party passes outside the opening. I stay put until late afternoon, finally venturing out like a bear after hibernation.

Once in the open air, it takes a bit for my eyes to adjust to the light. My back cracks as I stretch and shake the numb tingling from my arms.

No one is around. The search party must have gone home for supper. I head into the mountains, and it's nearing dusk by the time I reach the outcropping of rocks where Frank and I searched for Turtle Head's treasure months ago. Sitting on the smoothest boulders, I rummage through my bag and find a hunk of jerky. The dried meat fills me up, along with a couple swigs of water and a fig cookie. Before I know it, my eyes droop and my head slumps forward.

"I see some tracks up this way!"

The man's voice jostles me awake with a start. What was I thinking dozing off in the wide open like that? My heart clatters in my chest as I try to shake the haze from my thoughts.

More shouts from the men swirl around me like shrieking demons.

I have to think.

Hiding places are sparse on this side of the mountain. I listen a moment. The search party is coming from below. In a flurry, I weigh my options. To the west is barren. It's got to be a half mile to the east before there are trees tall enough I could use for cover. By the sound of their voices, I'll never make it in time. If I move north, I'll hit the canyon edge.

I shudder. My only choice is to head north and hope there's a spot where the canyon's drop isn't too steep to climb down.

Grabbing my supplies, I scramble the rest of the way up the hill. Sweat drips into my eyes, stinging them, but I keep moving. I escape over rocks and through prickly bushes. The terrain flattens the last ten feet before the mountain stops so abruptly it looks like Mother Nature sliced it off like a block of cheese.

Praying for a way down, I peer over the ledge. A sheer, one-hundred-foot drop greets my gaze. I study the cliff, hoping to find another option other than getting captured. I spot the place Frank and I lowered Josh over the cliff nearly to his death. It gives me an idea.

I run to the edge where ten feet below the cliff top the Cypress tree grows straight out of the wall—a splash of green on the gray rock.

"He's got to be close," someone yells from down the mountain.

I've only a minute before they find me. If I could hide on the underside of the Cypress tree, I'd be invisible to the men's searching eyes. Panic rushes through me. The cliff face is steep. Very steep. Chances are this is going to be the last fool thing I do in my lifetime.

Voices from below urge me on. There is no other choice. My hands shake like an old man's as I ease my way over the ledge.

In the dim light, I search for footholds and protrusion to help me climb. There aren't many. Climbing up a cliff is one thing but going down one is altogether different. I take my time even though my mind screams to be faster. For an instant, I take my eyes off the rock wall and glance down at the Cypress. Still another five feet to go.

"Randall," shouts a man. They are near the

edge. "Bring your lantern over here. From the looks of it, these prints are headed straight off the mountain.

I inch downward, every second brings me closer to my target and the men closer to me. My legs are tense, begging to feel something underneath them.

"Maybe the boy thinks he can walk on air." A rumble of laughter explodes from the search party.

Both of my feet slip and I fall straight into the tree. Sharp needles poke into me everywhere. My elbows, my ears, and especially my hands. I grab for anything I can hold onto to break my fall and then burrow deep into the gummy, sticky branches. The smell is pungent, a little like sage but more like a skunk. But I'm grateful for the pain and stink. The tree's dense growth blocks me from view.

"While I'll be," says one of the men, "you're right. The footprints go right over the ledge. You don't suppose he didn't see the drop-off."

"Might not have," answers another. "Stranger things have happened."

"You'd have to be a complete idiot to do that." Clyde Hampton's voice echoes into the canyon. "He might be a rogue, but I've never known Dillan Burnes to be a fool. I think we've been following the wrong tracks."

Knowing the Hamptons are part of the search party doesn't surprise me. All the same, I inch closer to the cliff where the larger branches offer more cover. In the rock wall in front of me is the crevice the tree grows out of. It's big—wider than two pickling barrels side by side.

I climb into the hole, and the men's bickering grows muffled. My breathing slows a little with the secure rock under my knees.

At last, after a good bit of hemming and hawing and cursing, their sounds drift away. Relief floods over me until I remember I'm alone, stuck in a hole, one hundred feet off the ground.

I scoot around in the cave, feeling my way about. It's much larger than I expected. A sharp pebble pierces into my hand. I pick it up and hold it toward the faint light shining into the cave opening. What I hold is not a stone. My mind whirls. Could it be what I think it is?

I fumble in my bag for a box of matches. I light one and hold the object I found close to the small flame. It's a ring with strange engravings along the side and a brilliant red stone set into prongs.

The match burns my thumb, and I blow it out. Patting the ground around me, I look for more jewelry but find only leaves, pine needles, and skeletons of dead animals.

Taking a second match from the box, I strike it on the cave wall. In its glow, I see an opening just big enough for a man's body to pass through. Blowing out the flame, I slither through the tunnel. Several yards in the walls open up. I've never been anywhere so dark. It's like looking into the heart of Hades. I pull a candle from my pack and light it. The wick explodes to life.

The glow reflects off of necklaces, bracelets,

earrings, crowns. The lot of it, every single piece, is gold.

"Why as I live and breathe." My words bounce off the walls. I'm standing in the middle of Turtle Head's treasure. Aztec gold. I'm rich. Filthy, stinking rich. The thought makes my legs buckle and I fall to the floor, surrounded by finely crafted riches.

My grandparents were right about the treasure. Wax drips onto my hand. "Ouch." I set the candle on the ground and open my pack wide. My breath comes in short spurts. I've never been so excited, except for when I almost kissed Ruth.

I know what I have to do. The people in town will band together to fight Preacher Docket if they knew there was money to be shared once the fight was over.

I put a few of the treasures into my bag—just enough to show the townsfolk the truth. I want to stay and count each gold piece. But I can't. I have a cliff to scale, an army to gather, and a mother to save.

21. NO FORMING CLUBS

FRANK and I sit on a crumbling rock wall that used to be a well. He holds a piece of the treasure I brought back with me from the cave. It's a band of gold that fits around his wrist like a piece of battle armor. He whistles long and low.

"You're kidding me. It was there all along."

I nod. "We probably walked by the spot fifty times during our hunts."

"I'll be a monkey's uncle." Frank runs his hand through his hair. "What are you going to do with it?"

"That treasure is part yours. Finding it was always a team effort. Question is, what are you going to do with that much money?"

Frank squints in the sunlight. "My brain doesn't know how to count that high. I'd probably buy me a third set of overalls, but after that I'm clueless."

"I want to build an army," I say. "One that can fight back against Preacher Docket and his hired thugs. Do you think any of the townsfolk would join?"

Frank thinks about it a minute. "I think so, though I'm not sure if they'd follow you. You're not so popular around here."

"How about if you help me ask them? I'm sure your family holds more clout."

Frank scratches his head.

"Come on, Frank," I say. "My ma is in jail. I have to do something."

Frank squares his shoulders. "You're right. We've got to do something. If people won't help out of common decency, then maybe they'll do it for money. Problem is the preacher has brought a bunch of men to keep law and order around here. A lot of folks are scared."

"I understand," I say, even though I'm disgusted. Preacher Docket doesn't scare me anymore. Well, at least not as much. Mostly he just makes me mad.

"There's no question that I'm with you...and my pa. He's had enough of the nonsense going on. Between the three of us, I think we could recruit a little army—maybe fifteen or twenty of us older boys and men. We'd still be outnumbered, but we'd have a fighting chance."

A small seed of hope grows in my chest, even though I know it's only the beginning.

———

Back in town, Preacher Docket has people working around the clock preparing for the Departure. I keep to the shadows like a fox waiting for a chance to steal a stray chicken. Over the last several days, I've only been able to talk with two men and three of their sons. But all of them were up for fighting. That's the good news.

It's near dusk. Every time I'm near the co-op, it's all I can do not to storm the make-shift jail on my own. I worry how things are for my ma inside. Apparently, there are nearly twenty other people being held. They are the ones who told Preacher Docket to his face they wouldn't go to Mexico with him. With that many people, you'd think there'd be some noise coming from within. But there's practically nothing, except for a young child crying out every so often.

Through a church window, I spy Mr. Hopkins unfastening the cross from the chapel wall. All afternoon he and his wife, the chorister, and another couple have been packing things that Preacher Docket wants to take with the group to Mexico. About a quarter of an hour ago, everyone but Mr. Hopkins left. Now is my chance.

I slip in through the back door. Mr. Hopkins doesn't hear me until I'm only a few feet away. He gasps. "Dillan Burnes?"

"I'm here on business, sir. Frank Worthen and his pa and I are putting together a group of men who don't want to go to Mexico, but who would rather stay here and rebuild the town. It'll take some fighting, and I'd like you to join. I can pay." I pull out a gold ring I took from the cave. "There's more where this came from. Some of it's yours if you join."

Mr. Hopkins' eyes open in amazement. He bites his bottom lip.

"Listen, I don't have much time. Are you interested?" I don't like being out in the open. It makes me too vulnerable.

"Who else is in?" His eyes are fixed on the ring.

"The Worthens, of course. Then there's Mr. and Mrs. Giles from the co-op, though Mrs. Giles will just be over supplies. Don Rowley and his two sons. Jim McFee, along with his son and neighbor, and the Atwood boys. If you and your oldest join, that would put us at fifteen, and I have other names on the list. What do you think?"

Frank had warned me Mr. Hopkins would be a little harder to sway, but if he joined us several others would come with him. He used to be a big shot in town.

He hesitates. "I...don't know. I'll need to think about it."

"No offense, sir, but you know as well as I do that Preacher Docket is raring to get to Mexico. There isn't much time for thinking."

Mr. Hopkins glances around the church, making sure we are alone, and then pulls me to the corner. His hushed voice is hard to understand.

"Listen," he murmurs, "I want to stay here. So does my family. But are you sure you and your band are a match for Preacher Docket and his men? I've no desire to go and get myself killed."

To be honest, I don't know if we're a match for the preacher or not. I could be completely deceiving myself that we've got a chance of even coming close to freeing Ma and the others. But the last thing I'm going to do is let Mr. Hopkins know that.

"There will be enough of us to take him down. Come to a planning meeting tomorrow night at the Worthen's. Ten o'clock."

Mr. Hopkins stares at the ring a minute more. "All right," he says, "I'll be there."

———

Just as Frank predicted, Mr. Hopkins comes to the meeting with several other men in tow, making our numbers almost twenty. Everyone is jittery and on edge. The feeling in the room is like a dammed-up river ready to break through.

Our main conversation is about deciding the best time to attack and where. We need to contain as many of the mercenaries as we can, and we need to do it quickly.

"If we hit them at dusk, we'd have darkness on our side. We know the layout of the town better than they do," offers Mr. Hopkins.

"But they're stationed all over at night. We'd have to pick them off two by two," says Frank's pa. "I say morning works better. A lot of them gather for coffee and a swig of whiskey outside the diner. With their hands full of booze, we might catch them off guard without their weapons ready."

"True," says Mr. Giles. "We could force them into the church and keep them prisoner there. The guards at the jail might be willing to surrender once they know their back up is out of commission."

We talk about it for another forty-five minutes, but in the end we agree that we attack Saturday morning. That gives us two days to prepare. I figure that's enough time to go to Smuggler's Hideout and leave a note for Josh and the midgets, letting them know what's going on, just in case something happens to me.

At the end of the meeting, Mrs. Giles tells us she's going to let the sympathizing women folk know to stay inside Saturday morning. "We don't want anyone hurt who doesn't have to be," she says.

Everyone agrees it's a good idea.

"Please don't forget to tell Ruth." Saying her name makes my throat catch. I'm embarrassed to let the other men know that I've got a soft spot, but no one seems to notice or care. They are all too worried about their own loved ones.

———

With a backpack full of supplies and pen and paper, on Friday morning I head for Smuggler's Hideout. I'll leave some food for Josh and the midgets when they arrive, and I'll let them know what's going on. If the army fails, it'll be up to Josh to find Ma. That is, *if* Josh is still around.

I scold myself for thinking such things. Josh will come. He will get better. As I wind my way through the branches, I think about what life would have been like if we hadn't lived in Dock-etville. Would Pa have died? Would Josh have gotten sick? One thing I do know is that Ma would never have been tormented by the likes of

Preacher Docket. The thought of his name makes me want to hit something.

Through the brush, I get my first glance of the cave. It's not a very pretty place, but the way it's tucked into the mountainside shielded with a maze of large boulders makes a perfect place to go to if you don't want to be seen. At times, Frank and I used to play out here as kids. We'd pretend we were cattle rustlers leading the animals to the opening to hide inside.

On the ground, I'm surprised to see a few footprints on an open spot of dirt. Instantly, the hair on my arms pokes up, and my breathing quickens. I crouch behind a large rock and tuck myself in. I can't be seen.

A moment later a familiar sight comes into view. It's George, gathering some dry kindling. My heart sinks. If he's already here, that can only mean one thing.

Josh is gone.

22. NO HORSEPLAY

"GEORGE!" I call, running, stumbling toward him. Tears blur my eyesight.

"Dillan?" he says, taking a step back from me.

"Is he…dead?" My body wants to split in two just saying the word. "Is Josh dead?"

"Why would I be dead?" says a voice from behind a bush. It's a strong voice. One that I haven't heard in a long time.

Josh steps out into the open. He's thin, but the color of his face is pink and glowing.

"Josh?" Fear drains from my body. My legs buckle and I fall down. Looking up at my brother, I realize how tired I've been. It's like my worry for Josh was the thing keeping me upright, helping me move, driving my will.

Josh plops down on top of me and begins to mess up my hair. "How do you like that," he says. "The sight of me was so intimidating it made you fall to the ground in awe."

"How long have you been here?" I ask, still stunned.

"A couple of days. We wondered when you'd finally show up."

I buck Josh off my back like a wild horse.

He falls to the ground, laughter spilling from him.

If I didn't know better, I'd think it was an angel singing. I pull him in for a hug.

"You look good, Josh," I say. "Really good."

"It was Edna's outhouse water."

"Her what?" I ask.

"Edna's water that smells like an outhouse," he answers. "I didn't think I could drink it, but she told me if I did, and if I really believed I'd get better, I would." He pounds his chest to show how tough he's become. "It worked."

"That's Edna for you. She can do everything with a little bit of smelly water and a lot of faith." George hands Josh the kindling, but before he can tell him what to do with it, George turns his head and cocks an ear. "What in tarnations is Behemoth bellying about now," he mumbles.

Josh and I looked at each other confused.

George turns back to us. "Josh, go get my eyepiece out of my saddle bag. Hurry."

Josh does as he's told.

George paces a few times. "Did anyone follow you here?"

"N-no," I answer. To be honest I'm not sure. I'd had so much on my mind about the attack on Preacher Docket's jail and freeing Ma, I hadn't thought much about covering my tracks.

Josh arrives with the eyepiece in hand.

"Give that to your brother," George says.

A lump grows in my stomach.

"Dillan, climb to the top of that tree." George points. "It will give you a clear view."

With rising panic, I run to the tree and hoist myself onto the lowest limb. As I scramble up the trunk, branches scratch my arms and face. Once at the top, I try to look through the eyepiece, but my hands shake too much and I can't focus.

Breathe, I tell myself.

Letting the air out of my lungs, I look again. Not too far in the distance, where the ground is dry, and the trees are thin, thick clouds of dust rise in the air. Men ride toward us on horses, carbine rifles in their saddle scabbards. My heart sinks to my shoes.

An ambush.

Someone told. I'd been betrayed. A flash of white from the approaching riders catches my eye. One of them isn't a mercenary. It's Nurse Mabel. She's probably coming to declare us legally dead when the job is done.

Me. Josh. The midgets. Four against nearly two dozen. We're doomed.

"Men with guns are coming," I call down. Shimmying down the tree, my mind spins with ideas. Should we head for higher ground? Hide? Stand our ground? Everything seems hopeless.

When my feet hit the ground, I explain. "Mercenaries who Preacher Docket hired are coming. They're armed and ready for a fight. We're outnumbered by...well, by a lot."

Arthur now stands at George's side.

I know what I have to do. "George, Arthur,

and Josh. If you leave now no one needs to know you've ever been here."

Josh shakes his head. "I'm not running."

"You have to." I rummage through my bag checking for my canteen for other supplies to give to him.

"I'm not leaving you," Josh says again.

I hand him my pack. "That should last you a few days. If you ride hard, you three can make it to—"

"You should listen to your brother once in a while," says Arthur, stepping in front.

"It's suicide to stay and fight." Why is this so hard for them to understand?

"Do you remember what happened to your red-haired friend when he tried to get into our horses' stall?" As Arthur asks me the question, George draws furiously on a piece paper with the stub of a pencil.

My heart beats loudly in my chest. "What? My red-haired friend? Oh, you mean Frank?"

"Yes. It happened in Docketville's barn. We doused your friend with—"

"—manure." I finish Arthur's sentence. "Yes, I remember. But we don't have time to talk about that now. You three need to get out of here."

"Listen to me, Dillan," says Arthur. "George and I are used to being outsized and outnumbered. We've always had to use our brains instead of brawn. Smuggler's Hideout is chock full of booby traps we've rigged here over the years. We don't have to give up. You just need to do as you're told."

George makes a few last marks with this pencil and hands me the paper.

"What's this?" I ask.

"A map of our traps," explains George. "Albeit a rough one that—."

"But what—" I try to interrupt but he doesn't let me.

"You're going to be the bait," says George. "All you need to do is follow the map and the instructions perfectly. It is essential for you to follow them perfectly."

"Josh, go light the fire," orders Arthur. "The fun is about to begin."

"A bucket of manure isn't going to do anything against this many men," I argue.

George shakes his head. "Do as you're told, Dillan, and we'll make it out of here alive. Now, we need to split up, which will divide the attackers into smaller groups. Josh, you head northwest. Dillan, northeast. Someone will meet you up at the slot canyon north of here. See it?" He points to it on the map.

I see it but don't understand. "Why would we want to meet there? The place is a bottleneck."

"There's not enough time to explain everything," George says. "Just remember, when you're in the trees don't go off the trail marked with cairns. Some of them are hard to see. Stay at least two feet away from the edge of Settlers' Bowl, and take the men chasing you through the slot canyon, not around it."

Josh has run into the cave. All of this seems like nonsense, but I listen.

Arthur looks at me. "You need to stay close

enough to the men chasing you so they can follow but keep out of range of their rifles. About two hundred yards should keep you safe."

"*Safe*? You're not serious? This is—" I stop talking because smoke begins to drift out of Smuggler's Hideout, making our position plain as day.

"What is Josh doing in there?" I say. "He's going to lead them right to us." Before I can bolt inside and give him a piece of my mind, Arthur grabs my arm.

"We can do this. How do you think we've gotten to be the most respected cattle ranchers around? There's more than one way to skin a cat."

I stop and stare. He has a point.

"Now go." Arthur slaps me on the leg. "Wait for the men on the hill over there."

———

Like a lamb to the slaughter, I wait on the hill until the mercenaries are closer. When they reach Smuggler's Hideout, I'll pop out of nowhere. The trick will be to make them think I'm running away, not leading them into a trap.

Smoke billows out of the cave. I hope Josh and the midgets know what they're doing. With the map on the ground in front of me, I take a second to study the trail. First, I'm supposed to wind in and out of the trees next to the cave. Next, I'll run by Settlers' Bowl, a steep, circular recess in the rock that looks like a bowl the size of a cornfield. And finally, the trail leads me down through a slot canyon where I'll completely lose my high ground advantage. What are the midgets thinking?

A coyote call from George signals the arrival of the mercenaries. For a split second, I wonder how much Preacher Docket is paying them. How much is their life worth?

The men burst through the trees next to the cave, expecting the element of surprise to be on their side, but they're disappointed. One of them hollers something in Spanish and points at me. I fake concern at being spotted and scramble away. Within seconds, a group of men on horseback are in pursuit.

I run, wishing I had eyes on the back of my head. I'm too slow. The riders are closing the gap too quickly. I speed up. The cairns lead me on a path that zigzags through thick trees, and the riders are forced to slow down. All I can think of is that I must keep two hundred yards between me and them, between me and death.

The first hint that something is happening behind me is the sickening bellow of a horse. Against my better judgment, I turn around. An animal lies on the ground, contorting in pain. The rider is at its side, coddling an arm that hangs limp. A trip wire must have caused the fall.

The second rider passes his injured companion without looking down and continues straight toward me. There's a look of determination in his eyes that tells me there's a bounty on my head. Behind the rider, some men follow on foot. I feel like David battling the giant Goliath. The odds are not in my favor.

The distance between me and the barrel of the men's guns is getting smaller. My curiosity has gotten me into trouble. I turn and run. My feet move quickly as my eyes search for the next cairn.

A blast from the rifle makes me nearly trip. A bullet whizzes by my head, and my heart pounds. *Keep going*, I tell myself. *Two hundred yards.*

The trail turns sharply. Two more shots ring out. Both miss. I'm the prey and they are the hunters.

I fear a trip wire might take me down as well, and I second guess the path, slowing my way. Up ahead is a dense grove of trees. A cairn is in front of it. I dash into the cluster. The trees are too close for horses to pass through.

As I run, the air seems to be getting scarcer, or maybe it's my lungs getting weaker. Panting, I exit the group of trees onto rocky terrain.

The bellowing from several animals fills the air. More horses are down. Hoping my pursuers are now only on foot, I breathe easier and slow my pace. I still have a ways to travel before Settlers' Bowl.

I steal a glimpse behind. Seven men are on my trail.

My feet slap against the hard ground, and I wonder how Josh is faring. Did the traps work for him, or has he been caught? Would they kill him here or take him back to Docketville?

I tell myself to stop thinking like that. In this game of cat and mouse, I must stay focused.

The open terrain is easier to run on; however,

the lack of trees gives the men behind me a clear shot. As always, the good and the bad go hand in hand.

At last, Settlers' Bowl is in view. I follow the map. To stay two feet from the edge I must hug the side of the mountain that the Bowl juts up against. I wonder why until I get to the slanted ledge and see that it's covered with small, loose, carefully placed pebbles. It'd be easy not to see the danger of the situation until too late. No longer do I rely on speed to stay safe. This is about precision.

I pick my way carefully, making decent time. Even so, the men get closer than they've been since the first time they spotted me. Two of them jump onto the ledge and immediately lose their footing. Head over heels they tumble down the fifty feet of slick rock into the bottom of the bowl.

"Ten cuidado!" The remaining men stop a moment and watch as I traverse the ledge. The one in front yells something to the others and then picks his way toward me, copying my movements.

My pace is steady, and eventually I'm on solid ground again. I hear another man behind me fall. Four are left.

My next destination is the slot canyon. The next fifteen minutes are all downhill. My knees shake and my energy slips away. The afternoon sun burns brightly, and my throat is parched. I look over my shoulder and am surprised to see only two of the men following me. Where did the others go?

The slot canyon greets me like an old enemy. I

turn sideways to fit into the two-foot wide, thirty-foot tall crack in the canyon wall. Being inside of it has always made me feel like I'm being shoved into the clothes wringer. Today, the feeling of claustrophobia is even worse because I know men with rifles who want to kill me will soon be in the same crevice.

The only way out is through the slot's opening on the other side. In the tight quarters, I stare straight ahead and slide my feet. First the right one, then the left. The back of my hand scrapes across the rock, making it bleed. I keep moving. There's no other choice.

It's not until I'm halfway through the slot when the men chasing me peer inside the entrance and shout, "He's in here."

I'm too far away for them to get a good shot. They'll have to come inside the crevice to catch me, and in this tight space, there's not enough room to maneuver a rifle. For now, I'm safe. My breath comes a little easier, and I keep sliding away from them.

Just when I think I'm going to get out of this alive, I see movement at the other end of the slot, near the exit. It's a person. Josh, maybe? I look more carefully and see there are two dark haired men. It's the other mercenaries. They smelled a trap and set their own for me. I swing my head side to side. Both directions are blocked. There's no way out.

23. NO LOADED GUNS IN TOWN

THE NARROW CANYON walls continue to close in on me. This was my fear from the beginning. It's like waking from a bad dream, only to realize you weren't sleeping.

I can't stand and wait for my attackers to get me. I want to face them like a man. Releasing my knife from its leather sheath and holding it tightly in my palm, I take a sideways step toward the men at my left.

You'd think a boy my age could die without regrets, but I can't stop feeling like I've left bread in the oven half-baked. Ruth. Ma. I wish I could have sorted things out. My one hope is that even with me gone, the rebellion will continue.

The crack in the canyon has become so tight, it renders the rifles of my pursuers useless. There's not enough space for them to lift the guns to their shoulders and take aim. The men abandon their firearms on the canyon floor and pull out their knives. Sick grins cover their faces.

In the middle of feeling sorry for myself, I glance up through the oversized crack in the canyon and look at the bright blue sky. There, snaking down the wall, is a rope. A beautiful, long rope.

I stop moving and wait for the twisted cord to reach me. It comes slowly. The mercenaries are now less than thirty feet away.

"Faster," I say to the rope as if it can hear me, but it doesn't obey. It continues to descend inches at a time. My hands are wet with sweat.

"Hurry," says the closest mercenary in a thick Spanish accent. Sneering, they move closer.

"More rope," I yell this time, and immediately it falls three feet to my waist. I wrap it around my chest in seconds. "Pull! Pull! Pull now!"

A force stronger than I expect yanks me into the air. The inside walls of the slot canyon tear at my exposed skin. I burn from the pain but still pray the rope to keep going faster.

One of the men slashes at my leg, slicing through my pants and hitting its mark. I kick him in the face, and he reels. Blood squirts from my wound, soaking my pants.

The scuffle gives whoever is pulling me up a few extra seconds to get me out of range of the other men's knives.

When I'm near the top of the canyon, I see something round fall past me and land in the slot canyon. Instantly, there are shouts and panicked voices. Several more gray objects fly down, and the men below scream in pain.

I grab the ledge and pull myself up the last few feet. Looking around, it's like I've landed in the middle of a circus. The rope wrapped around my chest is being fed through a makeshift pulley, attached to one of the midget's horses led by Josh. Not far from him, Arthur is dressed in a winter coat with the collar turned up along with a hat and gloves. He holds a hornet's nest, which he throws into the canyon's crevice.

The slot swarms with furious little black and yellow specks. A stray hornet stings my arm and I slap it. It feels like nothing compared to the throbbing knife wound in my leg. Below, however, the mercenaries are not so lucky. They clamor and wail as they are stung over and over by the raging mass of insects in the tight confines of the canyon.

Josh runs to me and throws his arms around my middle. "You're okay."

"What is all this?" I motion around me. "Did you plan all along to heft me out of the slot?"

"Of course. We figured by the third trap whoever was chasing you would get suspicious and try to cut you off." Josh spies my bloody leg, and he bends over to inspect it.

"Not now." I untangle myself from the rope. "Where's George?"

"He's already back at camp. The goose chase he led the men on was much quicker."

A few of the hostile hornets have found their way up the slot. I move away from them, hoping they don't call for reinforcements.

"Let's get out of here," says Arthur. He takes off the coat, hat, and gloves. His hair is wet with sweat under the heavy clothing that protected him from getting stung.

"But first," Josh insists, "we need to take care of that." He points to my leg. We take a minute to dress the wound while I tell Josh and the midgets about Ma being in jail and the town's plan to attack the mercenaries the next morning. Once the wound is cleaned up, we head back to Smuggler's Hideout.

Back at Smuggler's Hideout, George sits on a log. His rifle leans next to him as he whittles on a stick as if he's not got a care in the world. As we approach, he whistles two long notes and a short one. I've heard him do it before, but I can't remember when. A moment later, a furry rug the size of an outhouse lumbers from the mouth of the cave.

Behemoth.

The beast lifts his chin and bellows something that sounds like "hello".

"What's he doing here?" I ask. Seeing the bear makes me think of the night in the mountains when Josh and I thought we were going to be his dinner.

"*He* is a she," Arthur corrects me.

"And she," adds George, wiping the wood shavings off his trousers, "is doing a fine job of guarding."

"What's she guarding?" I move toward the cave.

"Take a look," says George.

Peering inside the hideout, I see more than half a dozen mercenaries and Nurse Mabel huddled in a corner. Everyone's hair is plastered to their heads, and something gooey covers their clothes. A sweet smell fills my nose.

Honey!

"Dillan Burnes," snaps Nurse Mabel, "get us out of this infernal place. We just came for a peaceful discussion, and we've been treated like common criminals."

Ma's lessons on chivalry are the only thing that stops me from laughing right in the woman's face. I do, however, let loose a grin.

"Stop smirking." Nurse Mabel wipes a glob of golden, sweet bear food from her cheek and stands up. "Obviously the bear is tame. I'm leaving this place!"

Behind me, the once-calm Behemoth curls her lips back and clacks her teeth together, all the while making a low, continuous growl. Nurse Mabel stops and slithers back to her spot on the ground.

Outside, I hear George and Frank saddling up the horses. I go see what they're doing.

"We've got a few hours left till sundown," says George. "We should finish this battle today while most of Docket's men are out of commission."

"You're right," I say as I limp toward my supply bag.

"I'll stay here with Josh and keep watch on the hideout and our prisoners," offers Arthur. "George, are you going with Dillan?"

"Yes, sir," he answers.

"But why do I have to stay here?" Josh whines. "I'm big enough to join the fighting in town."

I shoot my brother a look that tells him to hush, but he doesn't.

Josh complains the entire time we load the guns collected from the mercenaries onto the horses. He even stomps his foot and refuses to wave at me when George and I take off for town, but I ignore his antics. As I ride away, I think about how the next time I see my brother, Ma will be with me.

———

When we get to the outskirts of town, we stop by Frank's house and tell him and his father about the ambush. They both agree this is the time to attack. Together we gather all of the other rebellion members. Mr. Hopkins refuses to come, which is not surprising since talk among the men is that Hopkins is the one who revealed our location at Smuggler's Hideout to Preacher Docket's mercenaries.

In town, there are no fires lit at the blacksmith's, and the bakery's smokestacks are clear. Even the gnats, flies, and grasshoppers seem to have disappeared.

The quiet is enough to drive a person mad.

"Where is everybody?" Frank skirts alongside me on his horse. The whole group slows down.

"Rifles ready," George reminds everyone.

"I'll sneak around back of the co-op and see what's happening," I say. "Come when you hear me whistle."

As I inch closer, I'm relieved to hear voices coming from inside the jail. I hug the co-op wall and cock my head to one side. It gives me a clear view of the building. A painted sign on a barbed-wire fence surrounding the jail reads: "Abaddon: The Place of the Lost."

Sheets of plywood cover the windows. The door is reinforced and secured with chains and locks. Six men lean against the sidewalls and four more sit on stools near the front door.

"Shut your traps in there," calls one of the guards to the prisoners, "or we'll light up this place like a tinderbox."

The voices fade except for the sound of a crying child.

"Where do you think Docket is?" says one of the guards, scratching his dark, matted hair. "Shouldn't he be back by now?"

"He'll be home after dinner," answers the man to his side. "Speaking of dinner, Marco, go tell that woman we need food."

The guard at the man's left makes the sign of the cross over his chest. "I pray she's better at cooking than she is at being a nurse."

A ripple of laughter.

"And tell that woman to send any liquor she's been hiding as well," says the man in front.

Not one of the guards holds a gun. Instead, pistols are in holsters and rifles lean against walls. They don't know their reinforcements are out of commission at Smuggler's Hideout. I whistle to let the others in my group know to come.

"What was that?" asks one of the men resting in the shade.

"Not sure." The leader shakes his head and calls out, "Who's there?"

I count to twenty in my head. My backup will

soon be here. I step into the open, finger on the trigger of the rifle propped on my shoulder. "Hello, gentlemen."

Two men jump off their stools and reach for their rifles. I shoot a warning bullet that lodges into the side of the building in between the two them. "Don't touch those guns." I keep the leader in my scope. "Everyone raise your hands where I can see them."

The men slowly lift their arms into the air.

"You in front," I say to the leader, "throw your pistol into the water barrel. Now!"

He doesn't move. "You cannot make me. If you shoot me, one of my men will shoot you back."

I cock the rifle. "Do it now!"

"You're going to take on all of us by yourself?" The leader laughs.

"No," I say, "but they are."

My comrades come from around the side of the building into the open. Frank is there as well as his pa. Other townsmen follow. They all have guns aimed at the guards.

The mercenaries murmur and most raise their hands even higher to show their surrender.

"Keep your positions!" the leader of the mercenaries shouts, trying to keep control. "You won't get paid if you leave now." He blows a whistle, a call to his reinforcements.

"Your back up isn't coming," I tell him. "They tried to ambush us outside of town, but it didn't work. You're on your own."

"Liar." The leader turns his head and says

something in a muffled voice to his men. Several shake their heads.

"Then where are they?" I ask. "You gave the signal, but no one is coming."

"They'll be here."

We wait. Seconds feel like minutes. The silence is broken when the guard sent to get food from Nurse Mabel runs into the street. He's out of breath and shouting. "They're gone. No one is here." He sees us and stops.

The guards murmur in frantic voices.

I walk forward, keeping my eye on the leader. "Have your men with pistols take them out of their holsters and throw them into the water barrel. I won't ask again."

This time everyone follows orders.

Frank's pa urges his horse ahead of me. He calls out to the guards, "Everyone line up in the middle of the street."

A few of the guards separate themselves from the group. "Docket made us come. We are not to blame."

"I said in the middle of the road," shouts Frank's pa, motioning toward them. "We'll sort things out later."

Before anyone can stop him, the mercenary leader turns and runs.

"Get him!" hollers George.

Frank's pa slaps his horse and shouts like a banshee hot on the trail. The guards that remain stand on the road several feet apart and stare wide-eyed at their retreating leader.

Members of the rebellion tie the guards' legs

and arms together while Frank and I attack the lock on the jail's front door with the butt end of an ax. The clamor from the people inside is loud enough to split an eardrum. On the third try, I find my mark and the metal bolt breaks in two. The door heaves open from within, and a flood of people spill out.

Ragged men and women stumble into the light, squinting. Falling over each other in the wide space, they've forgotten what it feels like not to be squished together like animals in a pen.

"Ma!" I hunt for her face in the crowd, sickened by what I see: soiled clothes, parched lips, and sunken cheeks.

The mercenaries are all tied up. Members of the rebellion begin to help their starving neighbors. Over and over, they say how sorry they are that they hadn't done something sooner.

I cannot find Ma. I'm surprised, however, when Ruth walks out of the jail. She sees me and waves fiercely. "Dillan! Help! There's a child too sick to walk."

I follow her into the darkened building. It stinks of filth. A corner has been used as the outhouse, and the stench is enough to make me want to vomit.

"Here!" Ruth says, holding a toddler in her arms. "She's the Bates' youngest child. Her mother is not well. I'm afraid..."

I don't wait for the explanation. I take the little girl in my arms and run with her into the open air. Members of the rebellion are passing out canteens of water to all who are strong enough to hold it.

I find Mrs. Bates. When she sees me with her

daughter, she weeps. I set the young girl down by her and ask someone to fetch a canteen for them.

I hold my breath as I re-enter the jail. Ruth stands next to a woman who is trying to rouse her child from what looks like a near-death slumber. "Please," the woman begs, "please wake up." The boy opens his eyes and whimpers.

Ruth helps the mother stand while I hold the boy in my arms. The whole time my eyes scan the crowd for Ma. Where is she?

Then I see her. She's huddled next to the co-op wall, the thinnest, sickest looking of them all.

Ruth takes the boy from my arms and says, "Go to her. She needs you."

I run to Ma. She stands, wobbly on her feet, arms open wide. Her skinny frame reminds me of Josh when he was so sick, and it makes me shudder.

"Ma," I whisper, "let's get you some food."

"I don't care about eating," she says. "I'm just glad you're alive. Rumor was Preacher Docket killed you in the desert weeks ago. At least, that's what some of the recent prisoners said they'd heard."

"Lies," I answer. Ma's legs buckle. She needs rest and food.

I wrap my arm around her waist, and we make our way slowly around the co-op, heading toward the closest building with food—Docket's Hotel and Diner.

Inside the restaurant, most of the cabinets are empty, and the icebox only has a few eggs in it. On the counter, there are a few large plums.

Shining one on the sleeve of my shirt, I hand it to Ma.

She sinks her teeth into the flesh. "Hmm. They've been feeding us moldy bread and rotten vegetables—when we were lucky."

"Eat up," I say. "We'll find you more."

All of a sudden, Ma's face goes white. "What about Josh?" She turns her head around frantically.

"Doing better," I answer, trying to calm her. "He's at a camp outside of town. You'd hardly recognize him." It's strange. It's like Ma and Josh have switched places. Where one was sickly, now the other one is. I wish for the day when they are both whole and the family is back together.

Ma's mostly eaten plum falls to the floor. I reach down to fetch it for her when I see what made her drop it in the first place. Preacher Docket stands at the threshold of the door, dressed in his finest black suit, like Lucifer gathering the lost souls on the day of reckoning. Behind him is Clyde Hampton, and next to Clyde is Josh, who has a fresh gash on his forehead.

"Hello, Dillan," Preacher Docket says. "Welcome back."

24. NO SHOOTING VARMINTS

"JOSH!" yells Ma, clutching my arm like she might fall over.

Josh's face is grim. Obviously, the pride he'd felt earlier today is gone.

The sneer on Preacher Docket's face is as nasty as a hairy spider. Uglier too. "Dillan, I believe we have unsettled business," he says.

"I'll do no business with you." I've been so excited rescuing ma, I left my gun on the counter a good five feet from me. I want to kick myself for being as thick as two short planks of wood.

"Glad to hear you haven't changed." Preacher Docket waves a shiny pistol in his hand, one of those new fancy kinds from the city. His eyes land on my gun and he smirks. "You've been giving me some trouble as late. Men with broken arms and legs, hornet stings, and even a bear bite. But as you can see..." he motions to Josh, whose arms are tied behind his back and his legs lashed together, "...when your friend Arthur wasn't keeping watch like he should, I managed to snag me a fish."

"Are you going to murder him like you did your own father," I ask the preacher. "And you —" I nod to Clyde, "what a useless coward to put Ruth in jail?"

"The only murderer in this room is you, Dillan." Clyde spits on me. "And as for Ruth, she's there for her own protection. We're going to get married soon."

Calmly, I say, "If there's one thing I know for sure in this world, it's that Ruth Ivins will never marry a weasel like you."

"She's mine!" Clyde leaps into the air and knocks my head against the wall. He clenches his hands around my neck and starts to squeeze.

I raise my arms in between his and break his hold with a swift upward movement. A quick knee to his ribs doubles him over. Standing up, I ball my fists.

He surprises me with a swift kick to my injured leg. Angry spasms shoot through my body, and I groan.

"Hurts, huh?" he taunts. "How about this." Rearing back, he tries to land a blow to the same spot, but this time I spin around, elbows out. My right one connects with his nose, and blood spurts out, spraying both of us.

He bends down, clutching his face. I think he's trying to catch his breath when a moment later he launches forward and headbutts me. I fly backward, landing on my backside.

Something inside me explodes. Images flash through my mind. I think of all the times I've cowered to injustices in this town. Watching Ruth's hair be cut. Carrying a pig for miles. Being chased by men wanting to kill me. I'm always on the defensive. Never taking the lead.

I stand up, collected on the outside but erupting inside. Never again will I run.

Clyde approaches me and attempts a punch. With reflexes like a striking rattler, I stop his hand, clench it in mine, and twist. His shoulder wrenches and he screams in pain.

I grab his leg and arm, lift him up and throw him across the room. His eyes grow wide as he lands with a thud. In three large steps, I tower above him. A hard kick to his side and he rolls onto his stomach. I step on the back of his head pin him to the floor. Pulling his arm behind him, I yank it taut. One more pull, and it will break.

"Please," he begs, "don't do it."

From across the small room, Preacher Docket clears his throat in his condescending way. "I wouldn't do that if I were you."

Glancing up, I see the pistol in the preacher's hand. It's aimed at me.

Ma and Josh both cry out.

"I've had quite enough of you, Dillan Burnes," says Preacher Docket. "Not only did you take the life of my father, but you led a rebellion against my loyal followers. Your family has been a thorn in my side since the day you grandparents arrived in this town. You have brought nothing but misery to this God-fearing community."

Every part of me shakes with hatred. "You're the one who has brought shame to Docketville.

Your father would roll over in his grave if he knew what you've done. You hate my family because my ma wouldn't return your affections and run away to Mexico with you."

The gun Preacher Docket holds shakes slightly. "My father is dead because of you, and we all know what the Bible says about killing. An eye for an eye. A life for a life. Your treacherous soul has had this coming for a long time."

Preacher Docket aims the pistol. My skin chills. Below me Clyde groans. I take my foot off of his head. He's only been a pawn for Preacher Docket. I know that now.

My eyes dart to my gun on the counter. It's too far to reach, and I have no doubt the preacher will shoot me in cold blood.

But he doesn't shoot me. Instead, he turns the gun toward my brother.

Blood pulses into my legs and I leap, snarling like a cornered animal.

Preacher Docket fires the pistol once. I hear Josh scream. At the same time, my body slams into the preacher's. I try to pry the weapon from his hand, but he turns the nozzle toward my chest. Inches apart, face-to-face, we both struggle for control of the gun. We're so close I see beads of sweat on the preacher's forehead drip into his eyes. He grunts as I force his wrist the opposite direction, so the barrel is away from me. Another shot rings out. The gun drops.

Instinct kicks in. I pounce on the pistol and grab it. The metal trigger feels like it could burn my finger, like a branding iron ready to make its mark. I'm ready to kill the man I hate more than anything.

Behind me, I hear Josh moan loudly. I spin around to see his body in a tangled heap on the floor. His shirt is sopped in blood. Eyelids flutter. For a moment it's just the two of us—staying up late talking, pinching each other in church to stay awake, walking over rugged mountain passes.

Brothers.

I want to reach out to him, but I have unfinished business. I turn back around to find Preacher Docket is curled up on the floor like a newborn baby.

The weasel. He can't even face me.

"Any last words?" I ask him.

He says nothing.

My heart swims in hate.

"Well...I've something I want to say to you. May the devil have your soul." Now it's my turn. I cock the gun.

I want to kill him.

But...I can't pull the trigger. No matter how hard I try, my finger doesn't move. I drop the gun.

Preacher Docket's rule number 24 sounds in my mind.

No shooting varmints.

I guess some rules aren't meant to be broken.

EPILOGUE

ONLY TWO OF us sit in our pew at church that used to seat my family of four. It's been three days since the rebellion. Three days since I freed Ma from jail. Three days since Preacher Docket shot Josh. But really, it's been an eternity.

Frank's pa conducts the funeral services. The guilt and shame in the room are strong enough to taste. He clutches the pulpit. "Let's not forget Docket Senior and why he created Docketville to begin with. His vision was simple. Perhaps a little too simple, but his heart was in the right place. It's now up to us to find a way to begin again."

A few in the congregation clap.

"There's no reason to fester too much over those who hurt us," he continues. "I say, let God be their judge."

I'm too restless to listen to much more. I lean over and ask Ma, "Do you suppose we should have left Josh at home? You think he's all right?"

Ma shushes me. "He's fine. It was a clean wound. His shoulder will get better. Trust me."

"I should have stayed there to make sure he was okay." I reach over and adjust the sweater around Ma's thin shoulders.

"For the hundredth time, you needed to come here. When they close the coffin lid, it's over between you and Preacher Docket. You have too much to do in life to wallow in anger."

Frank's pa speaks again. "Preacher Docket lies before us dead, shot by his own hand while trying to kill another. There's a lesson there to be learned."

My mind reels back to the fight for the gun with Preacher Docket. At the time, I hadn't realized the bullet from the misfire had entered his chest and planted itself in his lungs. I'd been so full of anger I hadn't seen anything but hatred.

In my pocket, I finger the golden ring that was part of the Aztec treasure I found. I steal a look at Ruth who blushes and bashfully turns away.

I fidget on the bench. When will Frank's pa stop talking about forgiveness? Ma already told me I have to forgive or the hatred will rot out my heart. I know I'll get there...but it may take a spell.

Under the tree in front of the chapel, the townsfolk mingle, nibbling on burnt-butter cookies and other desserts that Mrs. Giles and a few other women from the co-op made. In timid voices, they ask each other about the future. Some know their plans. Others are unsure.

Surprised, I see George and Arthur ride up on their horses. Behind one of their horses is a one-person chariot they've rigged up in which Josh sits, propped up by blankets. He smiles when he sees us. Ma and I laugh.

I run to the makeshift cart and pull Josh out, careful of his injured shoulder. He holds me a few extra seconds and I relish them. His body feels solid and strong—such a difference from when I carried him on my back in the wilderness.

"We heard there was food," exclaims Arthur, jumping from his horse. Within seconds, he and his brother are stuffing their mouths full of sweets, joking loudly they must fill their bellies before leaving to run cattle later that day. They'll soon be off on their adventures, and I'll miss them. Giants among men.

Off to one side of the churchyard Clyde Hampton, his father, and a handful of their friends huddle self-consciously. A few in the rebellion had threatened Preacher Docket's cohorts with lynching, but a vote had been cast and the majority in Docketville agreed to let bygones be bygones. After all, we are all guilty, to some degree, of being bamboozled by Preacher Docket. We were all too complacent in Senior Docket's death. We were all too quick to judge our neighbors of wrongdoings.

Gratefully, the mercenaries have all gone from Docketville, splitting town immediately once news of Preacher Docket's death spread. The only person palpably missing in town is Nurse Mabel.

She hasn't been seen since Smuggler's Hideout. Some joke that Behemoth ate an extra snack that day. Others say Nurse Mabel jumped from the top of Settler's Bowl, too ashamed to face the town.

As for me, I think she's still out there. Hiding. Planning.

But I refuse to let my mind think on that horrid woman for too long. I have other things to keep me occupied. Much better things.

I walk toward Ruth slowly, and she gives me a sly look that makes my heart race. I can't stop myself from noticing how pretty she is. When I get next to her, she reaches out, takes my hand, and squeezes it. A smile covers her face. "I can't talk long. I need to get back to the house and help Ma with the cleaning."

"Hold your horses," I say. "I've got something to do first."

She eyes me suspiciously as I pull the ring out of my pocket. The gold band has a ruby red stone in the center. In the late afternoon sun, the jewel is the color of a ripe raspberry. I slip it onto her ring finger and look up, waiting for her squeal of delight.

Instead, she's looking at me like I just spilled a whole pail of sour milk on her.

"Will ..." My tongue grows the size of an overgrown gourd and my words jumble together. Taking a deep breath, I try again. "Will you be my girl?"

"Dillan Burnes," she says, "where do you get off asking something like that at your age? You're only fourteen!"

"It's just a promise ring," I stammer. "Nothing more." I bite my lips and wish I hadn't been so bold, but that ring has been burning a hole in my pocket ever since I got the idea.

Her mouth twitches as she holds back a grin. She's doing it again. Always teasing me. It's about time to give her a dose of her own medicine.

"Well," I pull my hand and the ring back, "never mind. I'll find another girl who might like it more."

She pushes up onto her tiptoes and puts both her arms around my neck. Blood rushes to my face and my heartbeat echoes in my head. "I would love to wear your ring, Dillan Burnes." Her cheek slides across mine and our lips touch. My mouth presses hers back tenderly, unaware of anyone else in the world.

There's no Preacher Docket to stop us.

There are no Rules for Saintly Youth.

There's just Ruth.

And me.

Sharing a kiss.

THE UNBROKEN RULE
—WHAT'S TRUE?

Communal towns like the fictitious Docketville, also known as Utopian societies, have existed off and on in various locations across the United States for hundreds of years. These towns have been founded on religious, philosophical, and economic ideals. Some of the more famous ones were the Shakers, Brook Farm, and Arcosanti, a community in Arizona that still exists.

The liquid used to "mark" Dillan as a sinner is called Gentian Violet. It is a nineteenth century dark purple antiseptic dye used to treat fungal infections of the skin. It has been regaining popularity as medicine in the twenty-first century.

Josh's sickness was commonly called consumption. A more accurate name is Tuberculosis. Tuberculosis is a contagious infection that usually attacks the lungs. In the 20th century, it was a leading cause of death in the United States. Arizona had one of the highest death rates from tuberculosis. However, that is because many people who already had tuberculosis moved to Arizona in hopes of a "sun cure".

Josh and Dillan's grandparents were part of the California Gold Rush. This was a time in history when a large number of fortune seekers (about 300,000 people) moved to California between 1848 and 1852 to find gold in mines and in streams. Historians estimate nearly $2 billion in gold was extracted.

The characters of George and Arthur are based on real people. During the early 1900s, the "Greenough twin midgets" were well-known ranchers in the southwest. They built a very small cabin that still exists today, abandoned in the wild country of southern Utah with no trails or roads to it. The twin brothers' grave markers are located in the cemetery of Kanab, Utah.

In the story, Turtle Head Rock is a clue left by ancient Aztecs to show the way to Montezuma's lost treasure. The mythical Montezuma treasure, taken from Mexico by the Aztec warriors escaping the Spanish conquistadors, has many alleged hiding places. The Four Corners of the United States is replete with tales from treasure hunters as being where the "golden riches" may still be.

In several Native American cultures, a petroglyph, pictograph, or rock formation that formed to resemble an animal, such as a predatory bird or turtle, is believed to be a sign of wealth or prosperity. Some speculate these symbols have been left as clues as to indicate hidden treasure.

The recipe for Snail Syrup that Nurse Mabel

gives Dillan is a real recipe that people in the early 1900s used as a remedy for coughing.

In the story, Nurse Mabel prescribes "apricot nectar" for Josh to get better. While there is no record of apricot nectar being prescribed for consumption, there are many reports of doctors prescribing grape juice for people to get better from cancer. The "grape juice cure" was popularized in 1928 by Johanna Brandt, a naturopath from South Africa. It has never been proven to work.

In the early 1900s, the drug company Bayer made cough syrup (like the kind Dillan stole from Nurse Mabel). It contained dangerous drugs like opium and cocaine. They did not realize at the time that these drugs were very addictive. While the drugs did stop coughing, they made people even more sick. There began to be hospitals full of adults and even children who were addicted to cough syrup. Bayer stopped making the cough syrup.

The name of George and Arthur's bear, Behemoth, comes from the Bible and means "a huge or monstrous creature". There are many stories, both old and new, about people who have tamed bears as pets. There was a modern example of a pet bear spotlighted on the Oprah Winfrey show in 2010.

Preacher Docket wants everyone in Docketville to move to Mexico as part of "The Departure". In the late 1800s and early 1900s, Mexico was considered a place of refuge for people wanting to get away from the laws of the U.S. government.

In the Old West, cattle thieves or "rustlers" would steal cows, hide them (in caves and other natural hideouts), and then take the animals across the border to Mexico to sell. Ranchers learned where the "hideouts" were and checked them often to make sure none of their animals that had been stolen were there. Ranchers used the hideouts themselves for protection in inclement weather.

Dillan runs into a slot canyon to get away from the mercenaries. A slot canyon is formed by the wear of water rushing through rock for thousands of years. It is much deeper than it is wide. Some slot canyons measure less than one to two feet across but are more than one hundred feet deep. Many slot canyons are formed in sandstone.

A LOOK AT: DUSTER

BY FRANK RODERUS

Saddle up with Duster Dorwood in this coming-of-age western from award-winning author, Frank Roderus...

With the end of the Civil War comes new hardships for 15-year-old Duster Dorwood and his family. After his father fails to return home and the urgency to provide for his family, Duster joins his first cattle drive, but when the job proves to be more dangerous than he thought... it just might be the death of him.

The young greenhorn finds himself in the midst of narrow escapes and unexpected friendships but the question remains... Will he survive the harsh trail life, Mexican bandits, and a kidnapping?

Rescue comes from the most unlikely place—but will it come in time?

AVAILABLE NOW

LOVE A GOOD SNEAK PEEK? DOWNLOAD OUR WISE WOLF SNEAK PEEK COLLECTION NOW.

It's no secret that you love books as much as we do. If you join the Wise Wolf Books mailing list now, you'll receive our free Sneak Peek Collection that introduces you to seven of our hottest YA releases. Plus, you'll stay up to date on our newest releases, news and sales.

———

Thank you for taking the time to read *Disobedience*. If you enjoyed it, please consider telling your friends or posting a short review. Word of mouth is an author's best friend and much appreciated.

Thank you.

Lois D. Brown

ABOUT THE AUTHOR

Former Washington, D.C., news correspondent **Lois D. Brown** has turned her interests to mysteries of the southwest, appearing in television shows such as "America Unearthed" and "Myth Hunters." Her nine published novels include a crime series *Robbed of Soul* that is based on the legends of Montezuma's treasure.